D0113716

Special thanks to the wonderful people of
the Pacific Islands for inspiring us on this journey
as we bring the world of Moana to life

And a very special thanks
to Kalikolehua Hurley

Designed by Tony Fejeran

Copyright © 2016 Disney Enterprises, Inc.
All rights reserved. Published by Disney Press, an imprint of Disney Book Group. No part of this
book may be reproduced or transmitted in any form or by any means, electronic or mechanical, including
photocopying, recording, or by any information storage and retrieval system, without written permission from
the publisher. For information address Disney Press, 1101 Flower Street, Glendale, California 91201.

Printed in the United States of America

First Hardcover Edition, October 2016

3 5 7 9 10 8 6 4 2

FAC-020093-17237

Library of Congress Control Number: 2016940718

ISBN 978-1-4847-4358-4

Visit disneybooks.com and disney.com/moana

SUSTAINABLE FORESTRY INITIATIVE Certified Sourcing
www.sfiprogram.org
SFI-00993

THIS LABEL APPLIES TO TEXT STOCK

DISNEY

THE STORY OF

MOANA

A Tale of Courage and Adventure

Disney

THE STORY OF
M@ANA

A Tale of Courage and Adventure

Adapted by Kari Sutherland

Cover and interior art by the Disney Storybook Art Team

DISNEP PRESS

Los Angeles · New York

The Story of
Te Fiti's Heart

hen the world began, there was only the ocean. It was made of endless waves, with nothing to break their flow—until a beautiful island emerged: the mother island, Te Fiti.

Her heart had the power to create life, and she shared it with the world. The sea and sky filled with birds and fish and plants, and more islands were born—homes for this new life. People, too, came into the world, and everything was in harmony.

But in time, some began to covet Te Fiti's heart, for they thought if they possessed it, the power of creation would be theirs. One day, the most brazen of them all—Maui, a demigod of the wind and sea, a trickster—decided he would find a way to take it. He possessed a magical fishhook that gave him great powers; he could shift his shape into any creature and pull islands up from the depths of the ocean.

Voyaging across the wide sea, Maui traveled to the island of Te Fiti. He used his magical fishhook to take the form of a hawk and swooped down to land in the trees. Once there, he transformed again, this time into a lizard, and scuttled through the emerald-green canopy until he reached the mountain that held the heart of Te Fiti.

The mountain proved impassable to his lizard shape, yet

CHAPTER 1

Maui would not give up. Clever Maui chose another form, turning into a beetle. As such, he was able to squeeze through a tiny crack in the rocks and found himself in the sacred space where the heart of Te Fiti glowed.

Shifting into his human shape, Maui crept closer to the bright spiral on Te Fiti's heart. He wielded his fishhook, prying loose the stone at the center and robbing Te Fiti of her heart.

Yet as soon as the stone was removed, the ground began to shake and Maui had to flee, taking form after form—beetle, lizard, and hawk—to avoid the crashing boulders as the mountains tumbled down on him.

He raced across the island, finding that all the trees, flowers, and plants were dying around him.

Without her heart, Te Fiti began to crumble, giving birth to a terrible darkness.

Maui flew off a cliff with a mighty leap, using his hawk shape to reach his boat. He pulled the sail taut, but as he tried to escape the destruction, he was confronted by another who sought the heart: Te Kā, a demon of earth and fire.

Te Kā was a terrifying being, dripping lava, billowing ash, surrounded by rings of flashing lightning. Maui grabbed hold of his fishhook and launched into the air to battle Te Kā, but Te Kā struck him from the sky.

Maui was never seen again. And the darkness continued to spread across the ocean, killing life until the heart of Te Fiti could be restored.

Bouncing on her knees, three-year-old Moana looked up at the tapa cloth her grandmother held. The brown and red paint on it traced the form of the ocean, a fishhook, and a spiral stone sinking beneath the waves.

"Maui was struck from the sky . . . never to be seen again," Gramma Tala intoned. "And his magical fishhook *and* the heart of Te Fiti were lost to the sea, where even now, a thousand years later, Te Kā and the demons of the deep still lurk . . ."

One of the children next to Moana twitched nervously as Gramma Tala's voice grew soft and ominous. The older woman lowered the tapa cloth to her lap.

". . . hiding in a darkness that will continue

to spread, chasing away our fish, draining the life from island after island"—Gramma Tala paused, then raised her hands into claws, her eyes twinkling mischievously—"until every one of us is devoured by the bloodthirsty jaws of inescapable death!" She clapped her hands together with a loud smack, like a shark's mouth snapping closed.

Gasps ran through the crowd of toddlers and several children clung to one another, but Moana sat forward and clapped, her face alight with excitement. Gramma Tala beamed at her, then turned to the rest of the group.

"But one day, the heart will be found by someone who will journey beyond our reef," Gramma Tala said, her tone reassuring, "find Maui, deliver him across the great ocean to restore Te Fiti's heart, and save us all."

"Whoa, whoa, whoa!" The shocked voice of Moana's father, Tui, the village chief, rang out from the back of the *fale* as he ducked inside. "Thank you, Mother, that's enough!"

His bare feet thumped against the ground as he hurried to break up the storytelling session. Scooping Moana off the floor, he touched his nose and forehead to hers in a *hongi*, and she crinkled her nose happily.

Then he set her down and turned to Gramma Tala.

"No one goes outside our reef. We are safe here. There is no darkness; there are no *monsters*." Tui swung his hands, accidentally knocking against the side of the *fale*.

Jarred loose by his movement, several tapa cloths unrolled from their posts, each one bearing the picture of a different giant monster, all with mouths full of sharp teeth.

"Aaah!" The kids screamed and recoiled.

"Monster!" shouted one girl, leaping to her feet.

"It's the darkness!" shrieked another child.

"This is how it ends!" a boy cried out.

"I'm gonna throw up," a toddler whined, clutching his stomach.

"No, no," Tui said as he waded into the crowd, trying to calm them down. "There is nothing beyond our reef but storms and rough seas—*oof*!" A little girl had elbowed his knee as she scrambled to hide behind him.

Still shrieking, kids ran all over the *fale*, crashing into one another. Some even clambered up Tui himself, seeking safety from the monsters higher off the ground.

"As long as we stay here, we'll be fine!" Tui raised

his voice over the shouts of the children. But it was a lost cause; they were too scared to listen.

"The legends are true. Someone will have to go!" Gramma Tala insisted.

Lifting a toddler's arm out of his face, Tui turned to her. "Mother, Motunui is paradise. Who would want to go anywhere else?"

Of all the kids, Moana alone was calm. She stood, gazing up at a tapa cloth painted to show a beautiful lush island—Te Fiti. She reached out, as if to feel the leaves themselves, but before her fingers touched the cloth, another child barreled into it from the side.

"Aaah!" the kid cried as he ran past, his face covered in the cloth. Tui lumbered over to help— children weighing him down.

But now that the cloth had been tugged off its hanger, Moana found herself staring at the bright blue waves of the ocean through the trees outside the *fale*. Sunlight twinkled off the water and an answering sparkle lit up Moana's eyes.

Everyone else was so caught up in the chaos, they didn't notice Moana slipping away and trotting down the path to the beach.

. . . .

As soon as her feet hit the sand, Moana felt like she was being drawn into a loving hug. The warm sand slid between her toes and over the tops of her feet while the peaceful lapping of the lagoon sounded around her.

Something glinted at the edge of the surf, catching Moana's gaze. Curious, the toddler scrambled over to where the water was nudging a beautiful conch shell up the beach.

It was light orange, like a flower, and it shone as if it had been polished. The point of the cone seemed aimed right at Moana. She wasn't supposed to go in the water, but surely she could just crouch at the edge?

Moana bent her knees and was about to reach for the shell when a high-pitched squeak came from her right.

Wriggling free of the sand, a lone baby sea turtle had cried out. Between it and the ocean stood a flock of sleek black frigate birds, their sharp beaks hanging open with anticipation.

Moana glanced at the conch shell, which the tide was pulling farther into the sea. . . . She looked back at the turtle. It would never get through the wall of birds on its own. Spotting a palm frond lying on the ground,

Moana jumped up and ran to fetch it.

At first, when the shadow of the palm leaves fell over it, the baby turtle seized up, pulling its flippers and head into its shell as far as possible. But when no claws tried to snatch it up and no beak pecked at it, it slowly peeked out. Moana smiled encouragingly.

"It's okay," she cooed.

The turtle rallied, working its flippers and inching along the sand. Gripping the frond with both hands, Moana did her best to keep the leaves over the little guy.

Almost to the surf, Moana began to tire. The palm frond trembled as she struggled to hold it aloft. Sensing her weakness, one of the male frigate birds darted nearer, his red throat flashing in the bright sun.

"Shoo!" Moana waved the frond at him to scare him off.

The bird hopped backward, cawing in annoyance, but he and the rest of the flock stayed where they were, watching sulkily as the baby turtle slid into the water. They'd made it!

Lowering the palm frond to the ground, Moana waved at the turtle, and it disappeared into the sea. Suddenly, the surf spiraled away from her, pulling backward to expose the sandy bottom where the conch shell she'd seen earlier was now lying. The water seemed to be waiting for her to approach. Then it actually waved her forward.

With a happy squeal, Moana toddled a few steps and bent to pick up the shell. As she leaned over, she spotted another shell a few feet away, still underwater. Cradling the first shell, Moana straightened and gestured at the ocean, asking it to move back so she could get the next shell, as well.

Gently, the ocean receded, exposing a strip of sand with walls of teal blue water on either side. Moana clapped in delight. At the end of the opening, a wave curled up, beckoning her to enter, and as she walked forward, the water kept retreating, exposing more shells laid out in a trail. The ocean was giving her presents!

Giggling, Moana carefully balanced the shells as her pile grew and she wandered deeper into the canyon. She stopped in a little half circle, peering into the water around her. Gliding past was the tiny turtle she'd helped, its mother next to it.

Moana's heart soared with joy as she watched them swim into the distance. As if to thank her for her part in the reunion, the ocean swirled around her in a sweet embrace. The waters parted again and a large wave reached over her, twirling her hair playfully. Moana giggled again. Then she spotted something else moving toward her from deep within the lagoon. The round object sparkled and glowed as it danced forward.

A curl of water held it out to her. Her other shells forgotten, Moana reached forward curiously, dipping her fingers into the water to grasp the object.

Pulling it back to her chest, she gazed down in awe and traced the beautiful green spiral in the stone with one finger. What looked like hundreds of years' worth of sand had crusted over the rock, and even though it was small, the weight of it felt momentous in her hand.

"Moana?" Tui called out in panic, breaking the spell.

Sploosh! The walls of water around her spilled in, and a wave plucked Moana up and swept her to the shore, depositing her on the sand with a little pat on her back.

By the time Tui's large shape broke through the trees, the water was smooth and unruffled, as though nothing out of the ordinary had happened.

Wobbling in the surf, Moana fumbled and

dropped the stone the ocean had given her. Just as she turned to search for it, two strong arms lifted her up out of the water.

Clutching her to his chest, Tui gasped, "Moana! What are you doing? You scared me."

Moana squirmed in his arms as he carried her up the sand.

"Wanna go back," Moana said, trying to wriggle free. Couldn't her father see how much fun the water was? How amazing it felt to stand in the shallows, the sand slurping through her toes and the waves tugging at her body, begging her to come in and play? More important, if she could find that pretty stone, she knew her father would love it.

"No," Tui said firmly. He lowered her to the ground and knelt in front of her, his face serious. "You don't go out there. It's dangerous."

Moana stared into his deep brown eyes, then looked beyond his shoulder. Nothing stirred the blue waters of the lagoon. No waves curled up to tease her. There was no sign of the beautiful stone. The magical moment was over.

Still . . .

"Moana?" Tui was standing now, holding his hand

out to her. "Come on, back to the village."

She reached up with her small hand to grab his and let him guide her back to the trees lining the beach. But her eyes never left the sparkling turquoise sea, even when her feet hit the packed-dirt path to the village.

"Buh-bye-bye," she whispered, just before the lagoon disappeared from view.

"You are the next great chief of our people," her father said, squeezing her hand gently as they walked along.

Moana cooed up at him.

"Oh, yes," he said, "you will do wondrous things, but you must learn where you're meant to be."

Neither of them saw Gramma Tala slip down to the water's edge and brush away the sand from the half-buried glowing stone. Holding it carefully, Gramma Tala stood up, her eyes following the tiny figure of her granddaughter dutifully walking beside her father. A twinkle in her eyes, Gramma Tala smiled and opened her shell necklace, then tucked the stone inside.

When Moana was ready, Gramma Tala would give it back to her. Swaying to the beat of the waves on the shore, Gramma Tala danced back to the village.

Meanwhile, Tui and Moana had come upon a group of dancers who were practicing on the grass on the outskirts of the village. Moana's face lit up as she saw her mother walking toward them, coming from their *fale*. Sina had lovely long dark hair and kind eyes. But Moana's favorite part about her mother was her soothing voice, its low patient cadence, which seemed to roll over Moana and wash away any problem or worry.

"Hello, you two," she said, lifting Moana and wrapping her in a tight hug.

"I was just telling Moana how she would be spending the day with me," Tui said. He started to join in the dance, winking at Moana. In a series of complicated steps, he rapped his flat palm down on his thighs, his elbows, and his stomach, the beats sounding out a staccato rhythm.

Moana watched, her body swaying from side to side. Sina set Moana down, and the toddler started to dance, too. Smiling as Moana clumsily imitated him, Tui asked, "Did you know that this song has been passed down from our great-great-great-grandparents?

Every beat is a link to our past, to our ancestors."

"Every beat connects us all," Sina added.

Moana wobbled and Sina held out a hand to steady her. Then, waving good-bye to the dancers, Moana's parents led her into the heart of the village.

"We take care of one another here," Tui told Moana. "We share all the food we harvest and catch so no one ever goes hungry."

They paused next to a pile of ripe fruit laid out on mats. Sina took three bananas, passing one to her daughter. As they kept walking, Moana peeled it and took a bite, savoring its sweetness.

"*Bowk.*" Heihei, a little rooster, waddled out of a nearby *fale*, tripping over a taro root. Moana steadied him, and he started pecking at the ground, clearly mistaking the dirt and twigs for food.

Remembering her father's words about sharing, Moana broke off part of the banana and tossed it to Heihei, who gobbled it down greedily.

Just then, a group of women weaving baskets waved them over. As her parents chatted with the basket weavers, Moana plopped herself down and picked up a few loose fibers. The women's fingers expertly wove the strands into round bowls, but Moana's basket turned out a little lopsided—longer and thinner at each end, kind of like a boat.

Inhaling the pungent scent of fish, Moana looked up to see a fisherman walking by, his day's catch in a basket slung over his shoulder. She heard the calls of more fishermen on the water, returning to shore.

Curious to watch them sail in, Moana stood up and began to totter down to the beach.

"Whoa, whoa, whoa." Tui scooped her back up after only a few steps. Tossing Moana onto his shoulders, he moved with Sina past the clump of strong banyan trees toward the grand *fale*. The sun peered through their canopies of leaves, seeming to make them sparkle.

"What a beautiful day," Sina observed, waving at the tapa cloth makers in a *fale* nearby. The tapping of their mallets against the stretched bark made a steady drumming sound—*tap, tap, tap.*

"We have a fine village, with wonderful and friendly people," Tui declared, shifting Moana so she could take it all in. "We are safe here, and the island provides us with everything we could need or want."

Finally, stepping up into the grand *fale*, Tui swung Moana around and around before lowering her to the floor. Sina moved across the *fale*, picking up the beautiful headdress she was in the middle of making. It featured red, brown, and white feathers. Bits of shells and nuts were woven into a decorative pattern on the front. She sat, her graceful fingers starting to move over a pile of feathers and reeds.

Moana ran toward her, pulling up short when she saw the headdress.

"Would you like to try it on, dear one?" Sina asked, a twinkle in her eye.

Moana raised her eyebrows in surprise. She had never worn a headdress before. Her father only wore *his* for important village ceremonies, and that one was kept up high where Moana couldn't play with it.

Sina lifted the headdress she was making and set it on top of Moana's hair. It was much too big and slid down over her eyes. Sina laughed and gently removed it.

Tui joined them, resting his hand on Sina's shoulder as he gazed down at their daughter. "One day, you will wear the headdress of your ancestors, like me. And like all the chiefs before you." He gestured toward his large colorful headdress resting on the top shelf.

Eyes wide, Moana nodded solemnly. She had heard her parents say that one day she would be chief.

But she didn't know quite what that meant exactly. Her father's headdress seemed so high up. Would that really be hers to wear? She sat, trying to think about it more. Then her ears picked up a distant sound.

Outside the *fale*, beyond the trees, the water rolled up the beach, wave after wave shifting the sand like patient caresses from a parent, the soft shush of the surf a soothing song that echoed Moana's heartbeat.

CHAPTER 2

"**Not so fast, Moana!**" someone cried from inside a *fale* as she streaked past.

"Sorry, sorry!" the now eight-year-old called as she swung around the corner of the building, her hand brushing the wooden pillars supporting its thatched roof. But Moana didn't slow down. If she wanted to see the fishermen pushing off, she had to get down to the beach right away. Her pet pig, Pua, pounded along next to her, his hooves stomping the grass flat.

Straight ahead, a group of women were tying knots in a net, the ropes spread out around them like a blanket.

"Good morning, Moana!" one of them called.

Smiling, Moana waved and ducked into the trees that formed the border between the village and the part of the lagoon where the boats were kept. Her feet felt lighter, the smell of the saltwater electrifying her like a bolt of lightning.

WHAM!

Moana's face smacked into the wide chest of her father, who was returning from checking on the fishermen.

"*Oof,*" he grunted, his arms folding around her instinctively. "Moana," he said in surprise.

"Hi, Dad," Moana said.

Catching up to her, Pua skidded to an abrupt stop at the sight of the chief, knowing that the race was over.

"Hmmm, let me guess." Tui's voice was weary as he held her away from him to study her face. "You were headed to the water."

"No," Moana said, feigning innocence. For some unknown reason, her father frowned upon her trips to the lagoon. "I mean, yes, but I was looking for—er—for you!"

One of Tui's eyebrows arched skeptically, but he just *hmmm*ed quietly as he regarded her.

Moana fidgeted in the silence. Finally, she couldn't take the pressure anymore and she flung up her hands. "Okay, I was going to the water. But it's just so interesting, Dad," Moana explained. "It's never the same."

Gently but firmly, Tui pulled her to his side and tugged her back toward the village.

"You know what I find interesting, daughter dearest?" he said. "How our amazing island gives us everything we need." The chief paused next to a tree and tapped on its bark. "Just think about this coconut tree."

"The coconut tree?" Moana asked, her brow wrinkled in confusion.

Coming up behind him, Moana's mother looked bemused by the conversation, as well.

"Yes, this coconut tree," Tui continued, warming to his topic. "No part of it goes unused. It all has a purpose."

Stooping, Tui plucked a coconut from the ground and knocked on its shell—*thunk, thunk.*

"How many uses can you name?" he asked, passing it to Moana.

She ran her fingers over the coarse hair of the round fruit, thinking. "We cook the meat from inside and drink its water, too."

"Yes, yes." Tui nodded in encouragement.

Picking at one of the brown fibers, Moana continued. "And these fibers get woven into our nets." Moana's face scrunched up as she concentrated. "Ummm . . . I can't think of anything else."

"Well," Sina offered, gesturing toward the tree, "the husks make good firewood, and—" She seized a leaf and waved it meaningfully.

"Oh, yeah," Moana said, "and the leaves are good for making mats and baskets, or building roofs."

"Or tickling daughters," Sina joked, brushing the ends of the palm frond next to her ear.

"Eeee!" Moana cried, twisting away from her mother.

With a chuckle, Tui caught her up and hoisted her onto his shoulders. She was almost too big to be carried like that, but she loved sinking her hands into her father's hair and taking in the view. She hoped to be as tall as him one day.

Tui swept out an arm, gesturing to the village before them and the green rain forest beyond. "You see, Moana, if you just stop and look around, you'll discover just how amazing our home is. Happiness is right here."

Slowly, Moana turned her head, watching the

villagers—the men and women, young and old—
working and playing, their voices weaving together as
harmoniously as the strands of a basket. It was true: all
their expressions were relaxed and full of joy. Moana's
heart burst with pride as she thought about what a great
leader her father was. The proof was in the smiles on
their faces.

"Chief!" one of the men building a new *fale* called
out.

After setting her down on the ground, Tui patted
Moana's hair, then strode over to answer the man's
summons. Sina brushed her hand over her daughter's
dark locks on her way to join the group of tapa makers.

Moana gazed after them, enjoying the bubbling
sound of villagers gossiping and the smell of taro root
stewing. Some men stood nearby, stoking the cooking
fires. Several younger kids ran past, kicking a coconut
along.

As a toy! Moana thought, adding another use for
coconuts to her mental catalog.

Turning, she saw Gramma Tala heading toward the
beach. Just as Gramma Tala was about to pass between
two trees, she met Moana's gaze and beckoned with
her hand—an invitation to join her on the sand.

Curious, Moana followed her grandmother down to the lagoon.

When she got there, the older woman was already in waist-high water, twirling, her arms dipping and rising as she spun. New wrinkles creased her face as she grinned at Moana and gestured for her granddaughter to come closer.

Slowly at first, then more confidently, Moana waded into the waves, reveling in the salty tang of the air and the warm embrace of the water.

"Can you feel the tug of the undertow?" Gramma Tala asked. "It's like a dance partner, spinning you one way while the top of the waves push you another. The ocean likes to play."

Moana swung one hand through the water, her skin tingling at its touch.

"The ocean plays with you?" Moana asked. A long-ago memory wiggled in her mind—shells laid out in a line, walls made of water.

"Oh, I know what they say about me," Gramma Tala said. "I'm eccentric and love the water too much, but I believe once you find what makes you happy, that's a part of who you are. So I don't resist it, even if that means people think I'm crazy!"

Holding out her hands with a laugh, Gramma Tala reached for Moana and they spun together through the waves.

Later, as the sun set, they climbed back up the beach and sat on a fallen tree, watching the last light of the day spill across the lagoon and the ocean beyond in bold pinks and reds.

Moana knocked her heels against the log beneath them. "A seat," she said.

"What do you mean?" Gramma Tala asked.

"The coconut tree also gives us somewhere to sit," Moana explained. "Mom and Dad were telling me that every part of the coconut tree is something we can use. Just like everything and everyone in the village has a purpose."

"Mmm," Gramma Tala murmured. "A purpose can give direction, but the wrong purpose can lead you astray."

Moana frowned, thinking. What was *her* purpose? To be a good daughter? To be a great chief someday? Was that what Gramma Tala meant?

Finally, Gramma Tala spoke again. "Your father means well and it is good to hear what he has to say, but the voice you must listen to is the one that comes from within. Trust your heart and follow where it takes you."

She pulled Moana in for a hug, their heads touching as they gazed out at the horizon. Did her grandmother know that Moana secretly yearned to explore what lay beyond their reef?

Bones creaking, Gramma Tala stood and stretched her back, then bent to pick up half a coconut shell lying nearby.

"As for the coconut," she said with a smile, "maybe there are more ways to use it, waiting to be discovered. Perhaps there are more paths to follow than the ones we know."

Pressing the coconut shell into Moana's hands, she gave her a *hongi* before walking away. Moana stared down at the coconut shell, its interior hollowed out. Instinctively, she leapt to her feet and carried it to the water. She eased the shell into the waves and set it free.

It bobbed gently on the surface, rolling over the swells like a boat. Moana smiled as the tide tugged it away. Maybe that coconut was meant to travel new paths. Maybe she was, too.

• • • • • • • • • • • •

Years passed and Moana grew. Her days were always full. She'd visit the bustling village, helping with various tasks, often partaking in the lively discussions and dancing, Pua at her side. She'd spend time with Gramma Tala, listening to the older woman's stories. Her grandmother had aged considerably, relying on her walking stick more and more, but she was still a source of great comfort and strength for Moana.

The sixteen-year-old also learned more lessons from her parents—her father teaching her the ways of a chief, her mother teaching her the ways of their community in her calm and patient way.

But Moana's absolute favorite thing to do was head down to the beach. Her love of the ocean had not subsided, and seeing the beautiful blue water always lifted her heart.

One day, Moana wandered down to the lagoon, finding an isolated stretch of craggy rocks. She perched on a flat one, sighing contentedly. On a whim, she waved at the ocean as though she were greeting an old friend. A small wave curled up in front of her.

Moana paused, cocking her head. Was it her imagination, or had it almost waved back? A flash of orange caught her eye. Wait—was that a conch shell?

It seemed so familiar. . . .

She leaned forward for a better look and—

"Whoa!"

"Moana!" Tui cried from behind her, holding her back before she could tumble into the ocean.

"Whoops!" Moana said.

Her father stared at her, frowning, clearly disappointed that she was once again at the beach. A thousand thoughts seemed to run across his face. Moana waited, not sure what to say.

Finally, Tui held out his hand. "Come with me."

He led Moana away from the shore and through the trees, deeper into the island. Pua trotted after them, but as the ground sloped up and the dirt gave way to rocks, he drifted away. Ahead of her, Tui began to climb up the tallest of the island's mountains.

On top of the highest outcropping, Moana took in the deep green of the forest, the emerald patches of the taro fields, and the brown triangles of the village *fales'* roofs. Moana's eyes drifted over the land, then rose up to the horizon, where the ocean stretched wide, filling the world.

Her father's voice broke into her thoughts, drawing her attention back to the mountain itself.

"This way," he said. "There's something I want to show you."

Steering her up the path, her father hiked on and Moana realized there was one more curve up the mountain. She'd never thought to go higher, but then her feet usually carried her down to the shore.

The trail narrowed, so they had to go single file until her father stopped on a little shelf at the very peak of the mountain. In front of them stood a stack of stones reaching up into the sky like a ladder to the clouds.

"When we're young, we search for our purpose . . . for our place. My dear, *your* place is on sacred ground among chiefs. One day, when you're ready to embrace it—you will stand on this soil, like I did, like my dad did, and his dad before him," her father said. His voice was soft and full of emotion. Moana glanced up at him and then back at the carefully balanced rocks.

"And you will add your stone to this mountain," he continued, resting his broad hand on her shoulder. "You will raise our whole island higher. You are the future of our people, Moana . . . and they are right here. Not out there."

Her father tilted his head toward the ocean. He paused and, suddenly, the weight of his hand seemed greater, as if he were passing his duties down to her right there and then.

"It's time to be who they need you to be."

Moana looked up at her father's kind and serious face.

"What if that's not who I am?" Her voice wavered as all the fears of disappointing her family and people churned in her stomach.

Tui's eyes softened. He leaned down, touching his forehead to hers. His deep-brown eyes, only inches away, held no doubts.

"You will be a great chief, Moana of Motunui . . . if you let yourself," he said. Beyond him, she saw the stones of all the chiefs who'd come before, their legacies built one on top of another. What would she have to offer? What would her legacy be?

Moana was quiet on their hike back down the mountain. She could not stop thinking about her father's words. The village needed a chief's full attention. She loved wandering to the ocean, but if she wanted to be worthy of her father and her ancestors— if she wanted to do what was best for her people— then she had to keep her heart and mind firmly on the ground.

They headed to the council *fale*. Once inside, Moana walked over to the shelf that held the beautiful headdress of her ancestors, her father's headdress. Biting her lip, she carefully lifted it up and placed it on her head. It fit perfectly. As she looked up, she saw the sun glinting off the waves of the lagoon, but she turned away, facing her parents and the village beyond instead.

Tui and Sina smiled at her, their expressions proud. Moana inwardly vowed to do her best to never disappoint them. She would study at her father's side and learn to be as capable and strong a leader as he was, to make sure her people were safe and never lacked for anything.

The village was her home . . . and her future. She would earn her rock on top of the mountain.

The Story of the Greedy Fisherman

ucked away in the village lived two brothers and a sister. Tautai, the eldest brother, had inherited their father's fishing boat, and day after day he went out on the lagoon to fish. The younger siblings, Lalolagi and Masina, kept the house neat and worked hard to make their brother's life easy. But ignoring all they did, Tautai grew resentful of his younger brother and sister.

"Why should I feed them?" he scoffed. "It is hot out here on the water day after day, and they are lazing in the shade. I will not bring them any fish today." So when he had caught enough for himself, he lay back in the boat and slept until sunset.

When he returned to shore, his brother and sister greeted him as usual.

"Hello, Brother, did you have good luck today?" they asked.

"No, I did not catch much, and so I have nothing to share with you," Tautai said, holding up the few fish he had snagged. "After all, it is I who needs strength to go out and fish tomorrow."

His brother and sister lamented his poor luck on the lagoon but did not argue. That night they went hungry. The next day, Tautai again went fishing and returned with just enough for himself. After another day of this, Lalolagi approached Tautai.

"Brother," Lalolagi said, "perhaps you could take me with you on the boat and teach me to fish, as well. Surely the two of us could catch twice the fish."

"It is my boat. I will not have you on it," Tautai said selfishly. "You will scare away the fish, and then we will have none at all."

As the days continued in this fashion, the villagers took note of how Tautai was mistreating his siblings. An elder scolded Tautai, saying: "This is not the way of our village. How could you treat your family so? We all must share our bounty."

But Tautai just laughed and waved him off. So the villagers shared their own food with Lalolagi and Masina, taking care of everyone in the community, the way they always had.

Lalolagi and Masina were grateful to the villagers and helped them with their chores. But they longed to contribute their own food so they could repay the favor one day.

Lalolagi went to their elderly neighbor with a proposal.

"If Masina and I help you with your taro fields, may we have some of your crop?"

The neighbor agreed, for he had no children of his own and had more land than he could work by himself. Week after week, Masina and Lalolagi gladly knelt side by side with their neighbor, learning how to turn the earth and plant the taro. He showed them how to dig a pit to store taro for the future.

One day, Masina and Lalolagi were walking through the

forest when they scared a flock of birds. As they watched them flap away, Masina had an idea.

"Lalolagi, could we not weave a net to catch these birds, just like the fishermen use nets to catch fish?"

Lalolagi agreed it was worth trying, so the two siblings set about weaving a net together. The next day, they went back to the forest and quietly spread the net, then startled the flock. That night, they ate a delicious meal, sharing some with their neighbor. They offered some to Tautai, but their older brother glanced at the bird meat and turned up his nose.

"That is more bone than meat," he said. "I will stick to my fish." Secretly, Tautai thought the roast smelled wonderful, but he did not want to have to share his fish.

Storm season arrived with a series of furious gales, the wind so powerful that it was not safe to sail and the waves so frenzied that the fish were scared away from the lagoon. Day after day, the fishermen, including Tautai, were unable to catch anything. The villagers fell back on their stores of taro, but when Tautai asked for some, the elders looked sternly at him.

"Why don't you ask if your brother and sister will share with you?" they said.

Knowing he had mistreated them, Tautai was loathe to ask them, so he tried to forage for coconuts and sweet potatoes. But Tautai did not know the island very well, and the sweet potato he chose was unripe and made him ill.

"Brother," Masina said, coming to Tautai's side as he rolled on the floor. "What is wrong?"

Moaning, Tautai pointed to the sweet potato. Masina studied it and shook her head. "That was most foolish of you," she said. "That is not ready to eat yet! I can make you a soup to help, but please tell me, why did you have it in the first place?"

As Masina made the soup, Tautai admitted that he had not caught any fish for days.

Masina and Lalolagi looked at each other, then turned to Tautai.

"Brother," Lalolagi said, "we have plenty of food and are happy to share our taro and bird meat with you."

Tautai was ashamed that his brother and sister were so generous and forgiving when he had been selfish and cruel. He vowed that when the storms passed, he would teach them to fish. From that day on, the three siblings lived happily, sharing their food, and the villagers smiled to see harmony restored.

CHAPTER 3

Dawn was just painting the sky from gray to blue when Tui knelt down next to his teenage daughter's sleeping mat.

"Moana," he whispered.

"Uumph." She rolled onto her side, facing away from him.

"It's time to get up, my dear," he persisted. "There is much to do today. We have our village council."

Moana blinked away her dreams and sat up, stretching her arms over her head. She heard Heihei crowing outside.

"The village council is today?" she asked.

"Yes, are you ready?"

Moana rolled her shoulders back and sat up straight, smiling at her father. "Ready," she said confidently.

"Good," Tui said, his eyes sparkling mischievously. "Because today you'll be leading it."

Her eyes widened and she blinked at him. Was he serious? Excitement flooded through her. This was her chance to prove she'd be a great chief!

She'd been training under her father for a while now, learning how to find the best place to dig a new store pit or how to judge which fields would be most plentiful. Her favorite days were when they visited the coral gardens and spoke to the women harvesting shellfish and crabs, but her father never tarried long on the shore and would rush her away as soon as possible, as if he thought the waters of the lagoon still tempted her.

He needn't have worried, however. Moana loved the village with all her heart and purposefully focused her energy on learning more about it, figuring out ways to help it thrive. She did not let dreams from before distract her; now she actively avoided the ocean. She had spent her time trying to absorb as much as possible about her father's chiefly duties. It seemed there were more and more problems facing the villagers these days—from lack of rain to livestock getting lost in the forest—and her father came up with many creative solutions. She'd attended plenty of village councils, but she'd never gotten to lead one. Her eyes sparkled as she grinned at her father.

Chucking her under the chin, Tui smiled at her. "You'll be great. Although, you may want to fix your hair."

Moana's hands flew up to her head, where the black strands were knotted in a wild tangle. "Hey," she said, "at least I don't sleep on my face."

Tui rocked back on his heels, laugh lines joining the creases on his cheek from his sleeping mat. "Good point," he said. "Well, I'll go wash my face so you aren't ashamed to be seen with me. You're lucky. At least you have your mother to help you get ready."

Pulling a comb through her hair, Moana smoothed it into waves, then stood and shook out her muscles, warming up for the day. She could do this; she was ready. She hoped.

• • • • • • • • • • • •

"Snort, snort."

A pig's round snout nosed against her legs as she stepped out of the *fale.*

"Good morning, Pua," Moana said in greeting as he flopped down next to her.

The pig rolled over expectantly, his feet dangling in the air, pale stomach exposed.

"All right, all right," Moana said, kneeling next to him and scratching his tummy.

Pua grunted in delight, wriggling his body back and forth under her hand.

"What do you think? Am I going to do a good job today?"

The pig wagged his tail and hopped up, resting his front hooves on her.

"All right, let's go," Moana said, leading the way.

In the council *fale*, Moana found her mother tucked into an alcove behind a curtain. A formal dress was carefully laid out in front of her.

"Hello, dear," Sina said, kissing Moana on the forehead. She wrapped the dress around her daughter, tightly fastening the woven tiers of dyed reeds over Moana's usual skirt and top.

Moana brushed her fingers over the deep reds and pale yellows of the dress, admiring how much work had gone into it. Clearly her mother had taken exceptional care that Moana be attired perfectly for her first trial as a leader—she took a shallow breath— even if the dress was a bit constricting. As Sina turned to get the ancestors' headdress, Moana's eyes caught the lagoon in the distance, the blues of the water seeming extra saturated in the sunlight.

Now was not the time to be thinking about the sea. She needed to focus. Moana ducked her head out of the reflecting light and reached up to yank down a shade. The stiffer materials of the formal dress made it hard for her to maneuver, but she stretched up on tiptoe and the reed shade unwound with a snap, blocking the view.

From beyond the curtain, Moana could hear the banging of drums, letting everyone know the council would begin soon. She wondered how many would attend that day.

Her mother positioned the headdress on Moana's head and tied it tightly in the back, then spun Moana to face her.

"You know what I'm going to say," Sina said, her voice serious.

Moana nodded.

"Left-right, left-right, up-down, up-down, left-right, left-right, shaaaaaaake! And freeze!" Sina called out, and Moana bopped her head as instructed, ending with a huge waggle before holding still.

The headdress had stayed put throughout, and Moana and Sina shared a victorious look just as Tui shoved the curtain aside and burst into the small alcove.

Pausing, Moana's father eyed her with pride, then dove forward and grabbed hold of her hand.

"Let's go, let's go," he said, tugging her toward the curtain. "Left-right, left-right, up—"

"Already did it," Sina cut in.

Nodding, Tui swept the curtain back and hustled Moana out to the main area of the council *fale*. In her peripheral vision she caught the movement of the drummers along the side wall, their mallets rising up and down like the ocean's waves rolling toward shore. Moana gulped, a sudden burst of nerves overtaking her. She tried to quell the butterflies that were zooming around her stomach, focusing on the line of mats her father was steering her toward. *Please, let me do a good job,* she thought. *Or at least not do something to totally embarrass my family.* All the council members were standing next to their mats, respectfully waiting for her father to take his place. Unfortunately, Moana's usual spot was taken.

"Heihei," Moana whispered, surreptitiously

trying to nudge the rooster off her mat with her foot. Even with her toes digging into his feathers, the chicken seemed completely unperturbed and refused to budge. "You gotta move. *Heihei*."

Next to her, Moana's parents settled onto their mats. Sina then glanced up at Moana, wondering why she wasn't joining. Realizing her daughter's predicament, Sina nudged Tui, who immediately shooed the rooster away with his battle-ax. Heihei barely seemed to notice, slowly sauntering off as if distracted by something else entirely.

As she eased down onto the mat next to her parents, Moana's stiff dress poked into her waist. She tried to project a sense of calm confidence, but her fingers rubbed nervously over the grooves of the mat. Pua trotted over and lay down next to her, seeming to sense she needed a friend. She looked down and smiled at him gratefully.

Holding his staff aloft, Tui slowly lowered it, indicating that everyone else could sit down, as well. A tremendous rustling ensued as the council and people gathered took their seats. Just how many people were out there? Moana couldn't see very far into the audience, since all the *fale*'s shades were lowered, but

Gramma Tala's encouraging face was front and center, which made Moana feel a bit better.

All the drums fell silent. Tui turned to the audience, but before he could speak, the village announcer burst out.

"People of Motunui! Chief Tui—" he cried, sweeping his arm toward Moana's father.

"Thank y—" Tui began, but the announcer wasn't done.

"—of Motunui!" he finished, throwing out his other hand in an extra flourish.

"*Thank you*," Tui said firmly, then addressed the crowd. "As you know, one day Moana will lead our people. That is why I have asked her to lead her first council today." With a large smile, he held out the battle-ax. "Make us proud," he whispered, his eyes gleaming.

Moana returned his warm smile and closed her fingers around the ax handle, the straps around it making it easier to grasp despite her sweaty palms. She looked out at the expectant faces in front of her.

"Moana of Motunui!" bellowed the announcer, startling her so much that the ax slipped, nearly slicing off Pua's snout.

Grunting in alarm, Pua backpedaled a few steps as

Moana clutched at the ax to get it back under control.

She glanced at her father, who pantomimed taking a deep breath. Moana inhaled and exhaled slowly before turning back to the crowd.

"I am very honored today to be here . . . today." A ray of sunlight bounced off the water and glinted in her eye. Moana twitched. "Uh, so let's, uh, let's get it started. I mean, let's begin." Finding Gramma Tala nodding at her, Moana took another deep breath. "Who wishes to bring something before the council?" she asked.

The *fale* fell silent, the only noise the rustling of skirts as villagers shifted in their seats. Scanning their faces, Moana wished desperately for someone to speak up.

Thankfully, one of the villagers raised her hand.

"Yes? Vela. Please, go ahead," Moana said.

"Hi, Moana." Vela, one of the sweetest singers in the village, rose. "*Fa'amalo* on leading your first council. My question is about the chicken behind you." There was a stir as the other villagers moved to look at Heihei, who was pecking at the air. "He, uh, seems to lack the slightest awareness and/or minimum intelligence required for basic self-preservation.

Would it be more humane to just cook him? Thank you."

Moana stole a peek at Heihei, who was now walking straight into the *fale* wall over and over again.

"Well, sometimes our strengths lie beneath the surface—*far beneath* in some cases," Moana began. "But I bet there's more to Heihei than meets the eye."

Heihei, having given up on exiting the *fale* through the wall, had just wandered over and attempted to sit on the chief's battle-ax. Moana awkwardly nudged him away, continuing her thought. "And I know I'd miss him if he was gone . . . or eaten."

A few of the villagers chuckled lightly. Tui caught Moana's eye and smiled, clearly pleased with her answer. She let out a small sigh of relief. This was going well.

Moana saw another hand rise in the crowd. It belonged to Taumuamua, one of the island's farmers. "Yes?" Moana asked.

Taumuamua got to her feet. "It's the harvest," she said. "This morning, I pulled the taro from the ground and—" Digging into a basket at her side, Taumuamua raised up a handful of taro roots, their ends rotted and black.

The villagers leaned forward to peer at the vegetables, then swung in unison to face Moana. Out of the corner of her eye, Moana could see that even her father was looking at her expectantly, waiting to hear how she would respond.

"We will separate the diseased crops from the rest and find a new field"—Moana turned and scanned the map of Motunui on the large tapa cloth behind her—"*here.*" She pointed at unclaimed farm area on the north side of the island.

Taumuamua retook her seat, dropping the diseased plants back in her basket as the villagers near her nodded approvingly. Tui and Sina exchanged proud looks. Moana's heart soared.

"Anyone else?"

The *fale* was quiet. Nodding, Tui moved to end the meeting, reaching for the battle-ax.

Suddenly, Gramma Tala coughed. "What about the fish?" the older woman asked. She pointed toward a fisherman on the other side of the *fale*. "Lasalo, tell 'em."

A dour fisherman, Lasalo's face was earthy brown from years in the sun out on the boats. He shifted uncomfortably on his mat before standing up.

"Oh, um . . . yes . . . there is a problem with the fish." Lasalo's voice croaked slightly. "The nets in the east lagoon are pulling up less and less."

"Then . . . we will rotate the fishing grounds," Moana said boldly. With a quick nod, she looked out, waiting to hear the next issue that needed her attention, but Lasalo remained standing.

"Uh, we have," he said. "No fish."

"Oh, then we will fish the far side of the island." Moana moved to the map and pointed at the waters on the opposite side of the mountains.

"Tried," Lasalo replied flatly.

Picking up a charred stick, Moana drew a mark over the spot, then shifted it to the west.

"The west cove?" she asked.

"Worse," Lasalo grunted, and Moana crossed that off, as well.

"Tide pools?" Her stick hovered over them hopefully.

"Worse."

"The windward side—" she began, but Lasalo cut her off.

"—and the leeward side, the shallows, the channel. We've tried everywhere," he said.

Moana drew in a deep breath, wondering what else to suggest.

"If there's no fish, what are we going to eat?" someone muttered.

"It's almost the rainy season," another person chimed in, worried.

More and more villagers expressed their concern, talking over one another.

Soon the *fale* seemed to erupt with a sea of noise and panic, a stark contrast to the silence from moments earlier. Tui stood and gestured for the villagers to calm down, doing his best to mediate the situation.

But Moana's mind was elsewhere. She squinted at the map, focusing. She remembered something her father had once told her: every problem has its solution. There *had* to be one here. She thought hard as she stared at the map. All the waters between the island and the reef had been crossed off. The lagoon's resources seemed to be tapped, but . . .

Suddenly, it was clear! There was something they hadn't tried yet, a place where there were bound to be more fish.

"What if we fish . . . beyond the reef?" Moana proposed, tapping the map with the ax.

The villagers quieted down in surprise, hundreds of eyes turning to her as one. The heaviest gaze of all belonged to her father.

Reaching over, Tui firmly lowered her hand, ax and all.

"No one goes beyond the reef," he said, his tone calm but final.

"I know, but if we have no fish in the lagoon—" Moana began.

"Moana," Tui rumbled, his voice getting louder. The villagers looked from Moana to Tui. Clearly this village council had taken a turn. Sina stood, getting ready to intervene.

"—and there's a whole ocean out there," Moana continued. It seemed like the only option they had left if the fishermen had really tried everywhere else.

"We have one rule," Tui said, his voice bristling.

"An old rule when there were fish," Moana countered. When the situation changed, they had to adapt, right? That was part of being the chief—coming up with solutions, with viable new ways of doing things.

Her father exploded, his cheeks puffing up in anger. "A rule that keeps us safe instead of endangering our people so you can run right back to the water!" he shouted.

A tense silence dropped over the *fale*, as though everyone was holding their breath, unsure what to do.

Moana stared at her father, then looked around at all the gaping expressions in the crowd. Feeling a surge of anger and embarrassment, she turned to leave. Her face hot, she fled from the *fale*, feeling the weight of the headdress now more than ever. She wondered if there had ever been a more disastrous first village council in all of history.

The Story of the Village Heartbeat

 very morning, Papa Toa sat out in front of his *fale* on the grass, chopping up coconuts for breakfast. His friends and neighbors knew it was time to arise when Papa Toa's ax began to fall against the coconuts.

Thunk, thunk, thunk.

As Papa Toa grew older, he was no longer strong enough to haul wood from the forest, nor did he have the stamina for fishing out in the sun. Everyone in the village loved him and knew he was saddened by his limited state, so they brought him all their coconuts to chop.

All day, throughout the village, you could hear his ax: thunk, thunk, thunk.

One day, he was feeling faint and lay down to rest. A hush fell over the village. Without Papa Toa's steady beat, workers fell out of rhythm, their mallets and knives missing their targets.

Papa Toa's granddaughter, Tiale, was gathering reeds to weave into a basket, but when she heard the discordant smacking of mallets, she paused. As she listened, she realized she could no longer hear her grandfather's ax. Worried about him, Tiale dropped her armful of reeds and rushed to his side.

"Papa, are you okay?" she asked, kneeling down next to him.

"What can I get for you?"

"Some water, please, Tiale," he answered.

Quickly, Tiale fetched the water, along with some mangoes. By this time, everyone in the village had stopped working, and they were gathering in small, confused groups to discuss what might be wrong. Why did something feel off?

When Papa Toa had recovered, he sat up and looked around him.

"Why can't I hear anyone else working?" he asked Tiale.

"Oh, Grandfather, it is because they are missing your steady beat. Don't you know you are the heartbeat of the village?" Tiale answered.

Papa Toa's eyebrows furrowed, for he had never thought of himself that way. "If that is true, I better get back to work," he said, reaching for a coconut.

Crossing her legs, Tiale sat next to him, handing him each coconut in turn.

Thunk, thunk, thunk went Papa Toa's ax.

Beneath the roof of a fale, several women settled back in their positions around a stretched piece of bark. Up went their mallets and—bang, bang, bang—down onto the bark to pound it into tapa cloth.

On the edge of the forest, men picked up their knives and axes again and with a snick, snick, snick, they cut off branches from the trees and piled them up to use in building.

In the center of the village, the oldest of the men eased down to the ground in front of the drums and smacked their palms against them: dum, dum, da-dum, dum, dum, da-dum.

Thunk, thunk, thunk.

Bang, bang, bang.

Snick, snick, snick.

Dum, dum, da-dum, dum, dum, da-dum.

As the music floated through the village, some of the younger men leapt up and began to dance—slapping their hands against their thighs, arms, and chests to add their own beats, their movements echoing the drummers and tapa cloth workers.

Grinning, a group of older women clapped their hands and snapped their fingers as they swayed to the music while other women headed down to the beach and waded waist-deep into the water. The women used the ocean itself as a drum, at first gently tapping on the surface, then scooping one hand under and up while bringing the other hand down fast, smacking them together.

Thunk, thunk, thunk.

Bang, bang, bang.

Snick, snick, snick.

Dum, dum, da-dum, dum, dum, da-dum.

Smack, clap, snap, splash, smack, clap, snap, splash.

Picking up a coconut, Tiale rapped on it with the back of

an ax: tap, ta-tap, ta-tap, tap, tap. *When her grandfather needed another rest and sip of water, Tiale took over, chopping the coconuts just as he had done. He smiled approvingly.*

Then, as though in answer to the music of the village, a gust of wind rattled the leaves of the palm trees together and a boom of thunder sounded in the distance. Rain was coming and with it a good bounty of crops for the villagers. Papa Toa and Tiale shared a smile. There was no sweeter song than that of the villagers and nature working together.

Thunk, thunk, thunk.

Bang, bang, bang.

Snick, snick, snick.

Dum, dum, da-dum, dum, dum, da-dum.

Smack, clap, snap, splash, smack, clap, snap, splash.

Tap, ta-tap, ta-tap, tap, tap.

Whoosh, clatter, clatter, BOOM!

CHAPTER 4

Whack!

Moana threw a coconut in the air and hit it hard with the large oar she had found by the fishermen's boats. *Smack!*

Her anger had not subsided one bit—not when she had freed herself from her constricting formal dress and placed it, along with the chief's headdress, in her *fale*. Not when she had run through the village, Pua trailing behind her, his little legs working hard to keep up. Not even when they had made it to the shore, the breathtaking view of the sea spreading out in front of them.

Whack!

"At least you didn't say it in front of the village, standing on a boat."

Moana whirled around to see her mother walking toward her. Sina gave her daughter a patient smile as she approached. Moana picked up another coconut and sent it sailing.

"I didn't say 'go beyond the reef' because I want to be on the ocean," Moana cried.

"Yes, but . . ." Sina reached out and lightly touched her daughter's arm before she could pick up another coconut. "You still do. . . ." She gestured toward the oar in Moana's hand.

Moana eyed it guiltily, then turned to stare at the ocean. The waves furiously pounded the sand as if mirroring Moana's mood.

Now it was Sina's turn to sigh. "He's hard on you because—"

"—because he doesn't get me," Moana finished for her.

"No." Sina shook her head. "Because he *was* you. Drawn to the water. He took a boat, Moana, he crossed the reef. . . ."

"*What?*" Moana looked up at her mother in shock. She had never heard this story before.

Sina nodded. "And he found an unforgiving sea. Waves like mountains." She paused for so long Moana wondered if that was the end of the tale. But then her mother spoke again, softly. "His brother begged to go out with him, but no matter how hard your father tried . . ." Moana's mother paused again, the silence weighing heavily between them.

Moana's eyes widened in amazement, a mixture of emotions flooding through her. She had known she'd had an uncle who'd passed away when her father was younger, but she'd had no idea how. Now she could picture the scene in her mind—her father and his brother out on the water, tumultuous waves taking them by suprise, her uncle not making it back to shore. . . . She felt numb with shock at the life her father had once had before her, sadness for his grief. She couldn't imagine losing someone important to her.

Moana looked over to the village and saw Tui in the distance, speaking to some villagers. She saw a pain in her father that she hadn't seen before, in the way he moved slowly, thoughtfully—the burden of responsibility a weight hovering over him.

"My daughter." Sina spoke again, pushing back a piece of hair that had fallen in front of Moana's eye. "Sometimes who we wish we were, what we wish we could do . . . it's just not meant to be."

Moana suddenly felt very small. She turned to look at her mother, the woman who had always comforted her when she'd scraped her knee, when she lost her way. "If you were me, what would you do?"

Sina pulled her into a tight embrace. "We must make our own choices, my love. No matter how hard they may be," she said. Then, giving her daughter another wistful smile, Sina left Moana alone.

． ． ． ． ． ． ． ． ． ． ． ． ．

The midday sun was sinking lower in the sky, its brilliant rays reflecting off the water. Moana hadn't left her spot on the beach, her mind still swimming with all she had learned.

It was strange picturing her father out on the water. Why hadn't he told her about that part of his life? Or that he had once held the same dreams as her?

What had happened to his brother was tragic, of course. Moana could understand that her parents just wanted her—and the rest of the village—to be safe.

She also understood that she had more responsibilities than most, that the well-being of her wonderful village would one day depend on her. Her father and mother expected great things from her; her people needed her to take care of them and lead them. She did not ever want to disappoint them.

And yet . . .

Shhhhh . . . Moana tuned in to the sound of the waves lapping up on shore. She closed her eyes. If she was honest with herself, it was her favorite sound in the world. She took a deep breath, inhaling the salty air. No matter what she did or where she turned, the ocean always lay in front of her. It was the only place where she felt like herself, like the person she was meant to be.

Maybe her father had been right. Maybe she had suggested going beyond the reef because there was a piece of her that just wanted to be out in the ocean.

She opened her eyes, looking out to the horizon— the limitless possibilities that lay out there.

Including the possibility of a solution to the village's problem.

She stood. Almost unbidden, her feet took her farther down the shore. Some fishermen were clustered near their boats, shaking their heads and muttering over their empty nets.

Someone should go check, at the very least, to see if there were more fish beyond the reef. And why couldn't that someone be *her*? Why couldn't she do both—settle the restlessness in her heart *and* help her people?

Boom went the waves, curling against the reef more insistently now. The crash of the ocean called, its song tugging on her heart harder than ever.

Would she ever be happy if she never learned for herself how far the horizon went?

As the fishermen tromped back to the village empty-handed, the wind whipped Moana's hair, practically pushing her toward their abandoned boats.

She could picture herself aboard one of them, the wind filling the sail and carrying her across the ocean to faraway places full of wonder and adventure.

Something tapped her calf and she looked down to see Pua holding another one of the fishermen's oars in his mouth, offering it to her. A grin broke across her face and she patted him on the head as she took the oar from him.

Picking out a boat, Pua leapt aboard. Moana dug her heels into the soft sand to push the hull into the water. The surf slapped against the bow in a friendly greeting. *What took you so long?* it seemed to ask, ebbing around Moana's legs next. She guided the boat deeper, then pushed off, her toes kicking silt into the water as she jumped up on the bow.

"Whoa," she blurted, the boat wobbling beneath her weight as she crouched inside. Pua snorted and looked to her, his big eyes asking what to do next. Carefully, she made her way to the center, Pua scrabbling along behind her. Moana lifted her oar and thrust it over the side.

At first the boat glided smoothly as she paddled out to the rocks, but then the waves began to get larger and it was harder to steer straight.

"There's more fish beyond the reef," she told herself and Pua as she plunged the oar deeper into the water. "There's more beyond the reef."

She tugged on the rope to open the sail and the cloth rippled in the wind, flapping noisily like the smacking of the slap dancers back in the village. Letting out a tiny squeal of alarm, Pua eyed the sail nervously, but Moana gave him a quick smile.

A giant wave rushed toward them and Moana angled the boat to meet it. Up, up, up went the bow—over the top of the wave.

"Yes!" Moana cried. "Not so bad."

Beneath the water a line of silver flashed as a fish

darted past. Maybe she was right! Maybe she would find all the fish they could possibly need just beyond the reef.

Suddenly, the wind shifted and the boom swung hard, nearly knocking her into the water. Moana ducked to avoid it, but while her attention was on the sail, an even bigger wave crashed toward her, the water sloshing over the hull and almost tipping the whole boat over.

Yanking on the sail and digging in her oar as hard as she could, Moana was able to keep the canoe afloat, but as the spray cleared from her eyes, she realized Pua was not next to her.

Quickly, she spun and saw Pua's head just clearing the surface of the water, his front legs thrashing desperately but his heavier lower half starting to pull him down.

"Pua!" she cried.

Abandoning the attempt to control the sail, she frantically paddled toward her friend.

Splash! Another wave, more powerful even than the first two, lashed the canoe.

Arms flailing, Moana fell into the water, where sound was muffled for a moment. The ocean rolled her this way and that, but she could see Pua's rump starting to sink.

With a tremendous kick, Moana swam to him and wrapped her arm around his body, propping his head up on her shoulder. She hauled him over to the canoe and hefted him up onto the outrigger. Just as she was about to climb aboard, another wave slammed into the boat and she was shoved underwater again.

She sank down, down, unable to get her bearings as wave after wave crashed into her. Sharp coral scraped against her and her foot snagged in a crevice. Moana winced in pain, reaching down to try to free herself. The rocks were tight around her ankle, trapping her no matter how she twisted. Her lungs squeezed in agony. . . . She was running out of air.

This is not good, she thought. Black dots appeared in front of her. *I need to . . . keep . . . going. . . .*

A few moments more and all would be lost.

CHAPTER 5

Moana jerked back and forth, her lungs
burning, her mind dizzy. Suddenly, everything came
into sharp focus for her. Reaching out, she searched
until her fingers wrapped around the hard shape of
a rock. She quickly smashed it down on the coral
near her foot, splintering the coral into pieces and
freeing her foot. Kicking fiercely, Moana surfaced
with a relieved gasp. She let the tide roll her toward
the beach, pulling the pieces of the boat—including
the outrigger, on which Pua was still perched—behind
her.

She had never been so thankful to feel land under
her as when the sandy bottom of the shallows rubbed
against her toes. Planting the balls of her feet, she
trudged up the shore, pausing to lift Pua down from

the remnants of the outrigger.

Unaware of what a close call that had been and already over the trauma of being in the water, Pua happily nuzzled her face. Moana set him on the sand and he trotted off to chase some seagulls.

She couldn't share her friend's clueless happiness. Her foot throbbed and, glancing down, she saw a thin trickle of blood winding into the sand. How was she going to explain the injury?

As the tide washed more of the wreckage onto shore next to her, she was struck by an even worse thought: how was she going to explain what had happened to the boat she'd borrowed?

Looking around, Moana spotted the sail draped across the water, floating near the canoe. She waded over to haul the boat to shore. Bangs and dents covered the hull and with the mast split in two, it would never sail again.

"Stupid," Moana berated herself under her breath.

What had made her think that she, an untrained sailor, should be the one to go beyond the reef and look for fish? Maybe her parents were right—the ocean was too dangerous.

The thought of her parents made Moana's stomach

twist. She couldn't imagine how they would react if they found out what she had attempted . . . especially in light of the story her mother had shared with her earlier.

Something rustled in the bushes along the tree line. Someone was coming.

"Guess Lasalo's going to need a new boat," Gramma Tala said wryly as she emerged from the greenery.

"Gramma," Moana began, then stopped, not knowing exactly what to say.

She tucked her injured foot behind her other leg, thinking at least she should try to hide her wound, but to no avail. Though she was getting older, Gramma Tala's eyes were still quite sharp. She waved at Moana to let her see it.

Moana sat on the sand and let her grandmother examine her foot. Then Gramma Tala slowly fetched some leaves. When she returned, she used her walking stick to lower herself down and dabbed the leaves along the scratch, using their sap to seal the wound.

"Are you going to tell Dad?" Moana asked quietly. He'd be so disappointed in her if he knew what she had done. It would only confirm his suspicions that she was putting her own desires ahead of the village.

"If you lost a toe, maybe," Gramma Tala said with a shrug.

Wrapping the rest of the leaves around Moana's foot, Gramma Tala tied them with a vine. Moana felt better . . . until her eyes fell on the ruins of the boat again. Her gaze drifted to the sharp line of the horizon and the roiling ocean waves, which after her crash looked less inviting, each splash against the rocks of the reef reminding her of her failure.

"I think he's right. . . . We don't belong out there," Moana said, trying to sound sure. She pressed her lips together firmly and nodded. She would just have to convince herself that was true. "Tomorrow, I'm putting my stone on the mountain."

Gramma Tala peered into Moana's eyes, a skeptical look on her face, but she just *hmmm*ed to herself and sat back. Turning to the ocean, Gramma Tala inhaled and exhaled deeply, her expression serene. In the lagoon, a school of manta rays glided majestically around a set of boulders, and the older woman smiled.

"Okay. Well, then head on back, put that stone up there," Gramma Tala told Moana, her eyes still on the lagoon.

Shoulders slumping, Moana stood and headed

toward the village, but at the edge of the trees she stopped. Something tugged at her heart as she glanced at her grandmother communing with the ocean, her arms reaching toward the sparkling water. Moana's feet carried her back to Gramma Tala's side.

"Why aren't you trying to talk me out of it?" Moana asked. Her grandmother was the one who always told her to find her own path.

"Because you said that's what you wanted," Gramma Tala said simply.

"It is," Moana said, her voice hardly wobbling at all.

Without looking at her, Gramma Tala nodded, her gaze on the manta rays as they slid through the rolling waves. "When I die, I'm going to come back as one of those," she said. "Or I chose the wrong tattoo."

"Why are you acting weird?" Moana persisted.

A half smile crept across Gramma Tala's face. "I'm the village crazy lady. That's my job!"

Moana had never thought of her grandmother as crazy, no matter what anyone else believed. She loved her fiercely and was always in awe of how Gramma Tala knew her own heart so well and was fearless in following where it led her.

Gramma Tala always had something smart and encouraging to say, and right then, the way her lips were pursed, it almost seemed as though she was holding back from saying more.

"If there's something you want to tell me, just tell me," Moana said. She waited, then added hopefully, "*Is* there something you want to tell me?"

Slowly standing, Gramma Tala leaned toward Moana and whispered in her ear: "Is there something you want to hear?"

Without further explanation, she hobbled away. What could Gramma Tala have meant? Where was she going?

Intrigued, Moana hurried after her, catching up as Gramma Tala reached a pile of jagged lava rocks at the edge of the shore. Picking her way over the slippery stones, Gramma Tala never wavered, not even when water splashed over the rim and lapped against their ankles. She merely planted her walking stick more firmly and curled her toes around the rocks, moving slowly but steadily.

After some time, Gramma Tala stopped, resting on a boulder next to a cliff face, and turned to Moana.

"You've been told all our people's stories . . . but

one," she said, using her walking stick to lift aside a curtain of vines. Several large rocks were stacked behind it, blocking what looked like the entrance to a tunnel.

First the fact that her father had once sailed beyond the reef, and now this? *What other secrets will I learn today?* Moana wondered.

Gramma Tala poked the end of her walking stick under one of the boulders and started to heave against it. Quickly, Moana joined her, and together they shifted the stone.

"What is this place?" Moana asked, still incredulous that she hadn't known it existed.

"Do you really think our ancestors stayed within the reef?" Gramma Tala replied.

As the last of the rocks rolled aside, a gust of cold wind shot out from the tunnel, blowing through Moana's hair. She shivered.

"Oooooh," Gramma Tala said excitedly, her eyes practically glowing.

"What's in there?" Moana asked.

"The answer."

"To what?" Moana asked, wishing her grandmother would stop teasing her.

"To the question you keep asking yourself: who

are you meant to be?" Gramma Tala whispered. She turned away and pulled a torch and flint from her pouch, then lit the torch.

In there? Moana wondered as her grandmother handed her the flickering torch.

"Go inside, bang the drum . . . and listen," Gramma Tala urged.

Moana gave her grandmother one last questioning look before taking the torch and stepping into the dark tunnel. Finding the floor uneven, Moana was grateful for the light as she ventured deeper into the rock. All along the walls, water dripped down, but she heard something else, as well—a low rumble.

Rounding a bend, Moana edged past a wide boulder and found herself in a massive cavern, the roof seven times her height. At one end, a waterfall spilled down into a pool before tumbling out another exit. Its crashing was what Moana had heard.

"Oh, wow," she breathed.

Rows and rows of ancient voyaging canoes filled the cavern—more boats than Moana had ever seen, their wooden hulls gleaming in the light of her torch. Somehow, they looked as polished as if their builders had just oiled them down.

But who could have built them? And what were they doing there?

Moana wandered among them, awestruck at their smooth curves and tightly bound boards. The village fishing boats seemed rudimentary in contrast.

Next to the pool, Moana found a smaller canoe, perfect for one person to sail. Her fingers trailed along its side and she jumped aboard, feeling it balance perfectly beneath her feet. The boom swung out and Moana noticed what was beyond it.

It was unlike anything she'd ever seen—a huge boat made up of two canoes lashed together by an intricate series of ropes, a treelike mast rising from each hull and a wooden deck at the center. Eager to explore, Moana climbed up to the deck.

It was no ordinary fishing boat. There was room on board for fifty men.

As Moana gazed around, she spotted a large log drum resting on the deck.

"Bang the drum," she whispered.

Moving closer, she picked up one of the mallets and tapped it against the drum. Nothing happened. She banged harder, but again, nothing changed. Determined, Moana set her torch in a nearby holder, then pulled her arm back and swung it down to hit the drum with all her might.

BOOM!

The huge sail cloth above her unfurled with a loud smack, and the light changed—as though she were out in the sun, not surrounded by rock.

Blooming in her mind, so clear she could almost see it in the cavern, Moana had a vision of the boat beneath her cresting a massive wave, the island of Motunui straight ahead. She could picture each of the men and women gathered in the boat, all rowing and singing in unison.

Full of joy, they leapt ashore, but even as they built their homes and danced on the sand, they passed on the knowledge of the sea—the wind and sky, stars and waves all keys to unlocking its secrets. New voyagers set out, young explorers roaming far and wide, returning home with the winds when they were ready.

Moana blinked as the images faded, the bright sky and rolling ocean replaced by the rock walls of the cave, and the people disappearing from the benches around her.

Still, the truth was undeniable.

Her ancestors had sailed this canoe across the

ocean, from far beyond the reef. They had navigated by the sun and stars, known how to capture the winds and ride the waves.

"We were voyagers," she whispered in awe.

Leaping up to the bow of the boat, her arms flung wide, Moana shouted it: "We were *voyagers*!"

Voyagers . . . voyagers! the cave echoed back.

The Story of a New Home

hey came from the west, sailing along the last rays of the sun as they sparkled on the water. For three months they voyaged, marking their course by the sun during the day and by the stars at night.

On board were men, women, and children of all ages, surrounded by the seeds, animals, and tools they would need to begin a new home on an island they were sure was out there.

Cross-legged in the seat of honor, Matai Vasa, their master wayfinder, breathed in the salt of the air and turned his face to the wind. As he scanned the sea and sky, the curves of the waves and patterns of the clouds spoke to him in a language he knew better than any spoken one. His shell necklace shifted on his chest as he moved to adjust the sail.

With the sun slipping below its zenith on the third day, Matai Vasa's keen eyes picked up a smudge—really just a slightly darker-toned patch of air beneath some clouds—to the south. His heart singing, he steered his people to the island floating beneath that shimmer, its tall green peaks bursting out of the water like a school of flying fish. Circling the entire island was a reef, the coral embracing the land like a mother's arms— shielding it from the rougher waters.

Canoe after canoe slipped through the reef into the peaceful lagoon between the rocks and the beach, and Matai Vasa's people leapt to the shore, their faces aglow. As Matai Vasa climbed the sand, tiny seeds shook loose from his clothing, and the wind swept them along until they settled next to a ridge— to grow in time, under the sun and rain, into a banyan tree, its branches stretching wide, its roots digging deep.

Just as the banyan tree flourished, so, too, did Matai Vasa's tribe—building their village on an inlet, clearing fields for their crops, harvesting fruit from the forest, and fishing in the lagoon. They named their new home Motunui, and although they loved it fiercely, they continued to hear the call of the sea.

Year after year, young wayfinders studied at the sides of their mentors, learning how to understand the weather, name the stars, find the currents, and more. Everything Matai Vasa knew of the sea, he passed on to his protégé—the leader of the next generation of voyagers. And when it was time for the protégé to set forth on his first journey, Matai Vasa passed along his shell necklace, as well.

From the shore, Matai Vasa and all the villagers watched as the younger man climbed aboard the boat and guided the crew out beyond the reef. A tingle of excitement ran through them. No one knew yet what adventures they would have, what new sights they would see, but they did know that no matter how far they sailed, the winds would carry them back home to Motunui.

CHAPTER 6

When Moana burst out of the cave, the sky was pink with the sunset. Singing the revelation over and over, Moana bounded across to where her grandmother rested against the cliff face.

"We were voyagers!" Her body practically fizzing with exuberance, Moana plopped down next to Gramma Tala, who chuckled at her enthusiasm and nodded.

Even though she'd known it to be true, Moana felt a surge of excitement to have her grandmother confirm it.

"Why did we stop?" she asked.

Gramma Tala made a disgruntled noise. "Maui," she said, throwing her shaking hands in the air. "When he stole from the mother island, darkness fell. Te Kā awoke, monsters roamed the seas, and boats stopped coming back. To protect our people, the ancient chiefs forbid voyaging."

She stared into the distance, her tone pensive. "Then we forgot who we were. The darkness has continued to spread—chasing away our fish, draining the life from island after island."

Tilting her head, Gramma Tala looked up and Moana followed her gaze. All along the cliffside, the vines were turning black, their leaves withering. Moana reached out tentatively, but as soon as she touched one of the blackened leaves, it crumbled, disintegrating into ash between her fingers.

Moana stared at the top of the cliff face and looked around to the sides, noticing other plants that had started to sicken, their leaves as dark as if they'd been roasted over a fire. She remembered what the villagers had said during the council earlier that day—the blackened crops, the disappearing fish.

Was Motunui dying?

"*Our* island?" Moana whispered, her heart clutching in fear.

"But one day"—Gramma Tala leaned forward and took one of Moana's hands before uttering those familiar words—"someone will journey beyond our reef, find Maui, and deliver him across the great ocean"—she turned Moana's hand over and placed a stone in it—"to restore the heart of Te Fiti . . ."

"And save us all," Moana breathed. She stared at the stone in amazement, its spiral so familiar it sparked a long-buried memory.

"The ocean chose you." Gramma Tala smiled.

But Moana only half heard her; she was too caught up remembering the magical moment so long before— the ocean parting for her, playing with her, giving her shells . . . and this stone.

"I—I thought it was a dream," Moana said, turning the heart of Te Fiti over and over in wonder. Using her finger, she traced the shape of the spiral. As she did so, the water around the rocks spun into a spiral shape and the stone began to glow.

Moana gasped, but Gramma Tala just smiled.

"Nope," Gramma Tala said. "Our ancestors believed Maui lies at the bottom of his hook." She used her walking stick to point at the sky, where the constellation of Maui's fishhook glimmered in the twilight. "Follow it and you will find him."

Moana finally registered what her grandmother was saying.

"Me?" she sputtered.

Could Moana really be the one who was meant to find Maui and save their people? The magnitude of it began to sink in and she shook her head. She had no idea what she was doing.

"Gramma, I can't sail. I don't even know how to get past the reef!" Moana's eyes widened as she realized what she had to do. "But I know who does. . . ."

Moana just had to show him the heart of Te Fiti. Together, they could journey forth and save their people.

· · · · · · · · · · · · ·

The shades had been lowered around the council *fale* as night fell, but Moana could still hear the fearful voices of the council as she hurried up.

"More crops are turning black," someone reported.

"We won't have enough food," fretted another.

"It's happening all over the island," a third person grumbled.

"Then we will dig new fields. We will find a solution," Tui's voice rang out.

Excitement shivered through Moana. She *had* the solution! She had the answer to all their problems.

"We can stop the darkness and save our island!" she cried victoriously, bursting into the *fale*.

Silence fell. The council members, including her father, were looking at her like she'd sprouted feathers. Oh, right, she had to explain *how*.

"There's a cavern of boats, *huge* canoes. We can take them, find Maui, make him restore the heart." She held up the stone, its spiral catching the torchlight. "We were voyagers," she pronounced, pride filling her chest. "We can voyage again!"

Nobody seemed to know what she was talking about. But surely they felt the desire to sail stirring within them, didn't they?

She looked to her father, who was sitting in the center of the council semicircle. He, at least, knew the pull of the sea. But his face had darkened at her words—storm clouds gathering on his brow. As though they could feel his anger, everyone turned toward him, their eyes asking if he knew what his daughter meant.

Rising to his feet, Tui strode toward her, his lips pressed into a thin line. Why wasn't he listening? This was the answer—the way to save their island and take care of their people. Before she could explain further, his hand was around her arm and he was steering her back into the night.

"Outside, now," he ordered.

The cool air of the night slid around them like the water of a mountain pool, refreshing and smooth.

"You told me to help our people. *This* is how we help them!" Moana exclaimed as soon as they were alone.

For a moment, Moana thought she had reached him—that he would agree. But then his face hardened and he stormed past her to grab a torch from the outer wall of the *fale*.

"I should've burned those boats a long time ago," he said.

"*What?* NO! DON'T!" she shouted, throwing herself at him. Latching on to one of his strong arms, she tugged until he came to a stop. "We have to find Maui. We have to restore the heart!"

Uncurling her fingers, she held out her hand, the stone resting in her palm. As the moon shone down, the stone almost glowed. There was no denying it was the heart of Te Fiti. Moana felt it radiating warmth and life.

But her father regarded it as though it were a cold dead bait fish—not even worth eating. Tui snatched the stone from Moana and waved it angrily. "There is no heart! This is just a rock!" He hurled it into the bushes.

"No!" Moana cried, falling to her knees. Frantic, she searched through the greenery, but as her father turned away, the light from his torch illuminated something else.

"Gramma," Moana said tightly. Her heart caught in her throat as she picked up Gramma Tala's walking stick; she never went anywhere without it.

"Chief! Your mother!" One of the villagers sprinted along the path, calling out to them even as a conch shell sounded in the distance, its mournful song shaking Moana to her core. Something was very wrong.

CHAPTER 7

Moana and her father raced down the path to Gramma Tala's *fale*.

Please be all right, please be all right, Moana chanted silently, all other thoughts gone from her mind. The only thing that mattered was getting to her grandmother.

Barely slowing at the entrance, Moana leapt into the *fale*, skidding to a stop at the sight of her grandmother stretched on her sleeping mat, Sina at her side. Gramma Tala's cheeks were drawn, her breathing a shallow rattle. For a moment, Moana stared at her in shock. How could she look so sick? Moana had just seen her. She thought back to their conversations on the beach, at the cave. She realized she had been too wrapped up in her own problems to notice her grandmother's slow walk, her need to rest more often than usual, her shaking hands.

As Moana sank down on her knees next to her grandmother, her mother wrapped an arm around her shoulders, but that did nothing to alleviate the tightness in Moana's chest.

Entering just behind her, Moana's father surveyed the scene, and in his face Moana saw the same mix of fear and dread that was curling around her lungs. Tui turned to the warrior who had summoned them, an unspoken question in his eyes.

"We found her at the edge of the water," the man explained. His voice was soft, as though he knew they were all close to breaking and he was worried one loud word would crack them open.

"What can be done?" Tui asked, just as quietly. Sina stood and went to her husband's side, leaning her head against his shoulder.

As the three of them debated potential remedies near the *fale*'s entrance, something soft brushed against Moana's hand. Gramma Tala had stirred and was reaching for her. Wrapping her fingers around Gramma Tala's, Moana was startled by how thin and cold she felt. She tried to gently rub warmth back into her grandmother's hand, as though by warding off the cold she could hold off death, too.

Gramma Tala's mouth moved, but Moana couldn't hear anything. She leaned close so her grandmother could save her strength.

"Go," Gramma Tala whispered.

"Not now, I can't," Moana said. Her grandmother needed her; she couldn't leave.

"You must," Gramma Tala insisted, the words rasping out of her throat. "The ocean chose *you*," she continued, as though it didn't matter that Moana had never sailed beyond the reef. "Follow the fishhook."

"Gramma—" Moana objected.

"And when you find Maui," Gramma Tala said, her voice gaining strength as she gave Moana's hand a little squeeze, "you grab him by the ear, you say, 'I am Moana of Motunui. You will board my boat, sail across the sea, and restore the heart of Te Fiti.'"

Tears welled in Moana's eyes. "I can't leave you."

Reaching up with her free hand, Gramma Tala wiped the tears away, then patted Moana's cheek. "There is nowhere you could go that I won't be with you," she said. Pulling Moana's face down, she pressed it to hers in a *hongi*. "You will find a way, Moana. You will find your way."

Suddenly, a healer rushed in, his bag of medicinal

oils and plants slung over one shoulder. Moana's parents whirled to consult with him.

With a gentle touch, Gramma Tala drew Moana's attention back to her, tucking something hard into her hand. Moana ran her fingers over the familiar curve of her grandmother's shell necklace.

"Go," Gramma Tala whispered again before her head sank back to the mat and her eyes fluttered closed. Her face relaxed and her breathing slowed.

Clutching the necklace, Moana moved aside to give the healer room next to her grandmother's mat. Then, knowing there was nothing more she could do there, Moana stepped out of the *fale* and let the night wash over her.

In the sky, the stars of Maui's fishhook sparkled, and Moana remembered her grandmother's long fingers tracing their shape for her when Moana was a little girl, the two of them lying in the grass by the shore.

"This one is the top," Gramma Tala had said. "Then these seven curve down and loop back up. Most important, these two are the final barb, so no fish can escape."

A playful gleam had come into her eyes and

she'd twisted up on her side to face Moana. "You cannot escape, little fish!" Gramma Tala had cackled, hooking her finger into a claw and swiping it toward Moana's nose.

"Eeeee!" Moana had squealed, leaping to her feet.

They had chased each other up and down the sand, water lapping at their toes.

The stars in the sky blurred as Moana blinked back tears. She realized that her grandmother had believed that one day Moana would need to know that constellation. Gramma Tala's words rang in her ears: "The ocean chose *you*."

Taking a deep breath, Moana fastened her grandmother's shell necklace around her throat and then retraced her steps along the path to where she and her father had argued.

After a few minutes of searching, Moana found the round stone buried in leaves and brushed it off.

Opening up the two sides of the shell on her grandmother's necklace, she slotted the stone inside. It was a perfect fit. Her grandmother had worn the heart next to her own all these years, never doubting that Moana would one day need it.

Maybe this wasn't such a crazy idea after all.

Feeling confident, Moana hurried through the village, stopping to grab a few baskets. She loaded them up with coconuts and bananas. At the fishermen's hut she picked out a rod and some hooks, in case she could snare some fish out on the sea. Finally, she went to her own *fale* and rolled up her mat to take with her. It would be a bed at night and shelter her from the sun during the day.

As she stepped back down to the grass, she nearly ran into someone. Her mother's eyes swept over her and everything she was carrying. Moana stared at her, silently pleading for her to understand.

Wordlessly, Sina handed her a roll of rope that she had woven, her expression bittersweet. With a grateful half smile, Moana took the rope and gave her mother a fierce hug, then slipped out of the village.

She passed a banyan tree she hadn't noticed before; half of it was black, dying. How had she not seen the encroaching darkness earlier? The crackling dead leaves under her feet seemed to whisper, *Go! Go!* Moana ran, hurrying to the cavern of boats.

Moonlight filtered into the cavern through the waterfall, painting the boats with an eerie glow.

"Snort, snort."

Waiting next to the smaller canoe, Pua held an oar in his mouth, just as he had done earlier that day.

Kneeling next to him, Moana sighed. No matter how much she wanted to, she couldn't risk taking her little friend with her, especially after what had happened last time. She wouldn't be able to forgive herself if something happened to him. "I'm going to miss you, Pua. But I'll be back, and then I can tell you all about my adventures," she whispered.

After one final scratch behind his ears, Moana stood and slung her supplies into the canoe, then maneuvered it into the water.

"Auê!" she shouted as she paddled it over the edge of the little waterfall and out into the lagoon with a splash.

The boat coasted over the water, perfectly balanced, and once again Moana admired the craftsmanship of her ancestors. It seemed impossible that she could capsize this boat, but for all her passion, she *was* still a new voyager.

Was this a mistake? Moana's eyes turned back to the shore, where she saw smoke rising from torches and cooking fires in the village. Was she really going to leave everyone and everything she knew?

Her heart twisted as the light in her grandmother's *fale* was extinguished—a sign that her grandmother had joined their ancestors.

Maybe Moana should go back, comfort her father and give up this idea. Before doubt could overwhelm her, a glowing shape dove over the sand and into the lagoon. As it came closer to her, Moana saw it was a spectral manta ray—her grandmother's favorite animal—winging toward the open ocean.

A grin tugged at her lips as the ray's blue light zipped under her boat and flew over the reef, illuminating a channel through the coral.

"Thanks, Gramma," Moana said, picking up her oar.

Steering toward the rocks, Moana followed the path the manta ray had taken. Large waves bore down on her, but Moana paddled hard, then quickly opened the sail. With a *whoosh*, the wind filled the cloth and the boat soared over the reef like a hawk in the sky.

Yes! Moana raised her paddle in victory. She'd done it! As the boat gained speed, she glanced back to where, in the distance, Motunui was getting smaller and smaller. She'd come home again, once she'd found Maui, taken him to Te Fiti to restore the heart, and saved them all.

Facing forward, Moana angled the boat so the stars of Maui's fishhook were in line with the bow. The sail snapped full, harnessing the wind, and the boat lifted over the waves.

"Woo-hoo!" Moana called, blinking the sea spray from her eyes.

Hope filled her chest, like a second sail on the boat, carrying her toward adventure.

Out on the ocean, anything seemed possible.

The Story of
Vailele and the Whale

ong, long ago there was a fisherman named Vailele who sailed far out into the ocean, ostensibly for deep-sea fish. But the real reason was that Vailele was drawn to the waves. He would sit on his boat for hours, hardly bothering to cast his line, and just watch the water flow around his canoe, floating it this way and that.

One day, a sudden summer squall caught him on the open ocean and capsized his boat. Clinging to the overturned hull, Vailele prayed for help as the rain thundered down on him and large waves tossed him from side to side. Eventually, the storm calmed, but by then Vailele was far from his island.

As he drifted, summoning the strength to right his boat, he felt something large nudge against him. Then it came again. Terrified it might be a shark, Vailele scrambled up onto the hull before the animal could return.

Whhff! A round-nosed head broke the surface, and then a spurt of water blasted up and cascaded down on Vailele. Splat, splat, splat, went the droplets against the hull.

Vailele danced in delight. His visitor was a humpback whale! Sliding to the edge of the hull, Vailele reached out his hand and rested it on the water. Patiently, he waited as the whale dove down and circled his boat. As it passed by, the whale rolled onto its side, eyeing him curiously. Vailele held very still until it gently nosed against his hand.

He rubbed his palm over its bumpy, rubbery skin, then eased into the water next to it, wrapping his arm over its head. The whale wriggled closer, letting Vailele climb on top.

Once Vailele was aboard, the whale surged forward, its tail propelling them through the waves. Vailele clung to the whale, his face beaming.

The whale began to sink below the surface, so Vailele took a deep breath. Down, down, down they went—the water getting colder and colder. It was colder than the chilliest night back home, and a funny feeling crept into Vailele's fingers and toes.

Suddenly, Vailele and the whale were surrounded by a fast-moving stream of water. The current carried Vailele and the whale for a ways, and then the whale rose to the surface so they could both take another breath.

The deeper the water, the colder it is, *Vailele thought.* Fast-flowing rivers run through the ocean, too.

For miles, the whale carried Vailele through the ocean, showing him different currents and waves, until Vailele spotted land in the distance. Sensing his excitement, the whale took Vailele to the island. Its body shivered and shook as it touched the bottom, and Vailele slid off into the warm shallow water, sand squishing between his toes.

As he stood there, smaller curls of water washed over his legs. Vailele knew those ripples were the children of the waves farther out. Taking a deep breath, he smelled the salt of the sea mixing with the sweet perfume of plumeria from farther inland.

After some time, Vailele swam deeper into the sea to where the whale waited for him, and it sank below the water to rise under him so he could again ride it. Now that it had taught him of the currents and introduced him to the different waves, the whale carried him home.

Back among his people, Vailele told them of his adventures and of what he'd seen in the ocean. From then on, Vailele and his fellow voyagers had mastery of the currents and could recognize the waves.

And on every voyage he took, Vailele was accompanied by his friend the whale, its graceful back slipping through the water beside his boat like a second outrigger.

CHAPTER 8

Pinks and reds and oranges swept over the horizon, like someone had dipped a paintbrush in flowers and was drawing it along, with the clouds as their canvas, in the most beautiful sunrise Moana had ever seen.

Taking a deep breath, she rehearsed what she planned to say when she found Maui. "I am Moana of Motunui. You will board my boat, sail across the sea, and restore the heart of Te Fiti." That sounded pretty good already, but practice made perfect. "I am Moana . . ." She trailed off as she heard an odd noise.

Thunk.

Moana glanced around, but she didn't see anything. ". . . Of Motu—"

Thunk.

"—nui . . ." That sound had definitely come from within the boat.

Thunk.

Leaning forward, Moana peered past the boat's drum and into the cargo hold, where she'd stowed all her supplies. As she watched, one of the coconuts rose out of the pile.

"Ba-gock?" the coconut squawked.

"Heihei?" Moana said, reaching out toward the coconut. The rooster must have been sleeping in the canoe the whole night, hidden among the coconuts. But how had the village's most lovable pest found his way to the cavern in the first place?

As she lifted the coconut shell off his head, the rooster blinked up at her. His head swung to the side, perhaps searching for food, but he discovered only vast, open ocean waves—no land or trees in sight.

"Baaaaagh!" Heihei shrieked, his feathers springing outward in shock.

Quickly, Moana plopped the coconut shell back over his head, and the rooster immediately calmed. She gave him a moment to collect himself, then pulled the shell back off.

"Baaaaaaagh!" Heihei screamed again.

Down went the shell over his eyes, and he quieted. Moana waited a beat again and then tentatively removed the coconut. This time the rooster merely gazed impassively around. Unperturbed, he pecked at the coconuts around him, plucking up a few fibers.

Moana rolled her eyes. *Silly rooster,* she thought. But it was a good sign that he'd acclimated to the sight of the ocean, since it looked like they'd be on it together for a long time.

"There we go, yeah, nice water," she told him, scooping him out of the cargo hold and setting him next to her. "The ocean's actually a friend of mine."

Cocking his head, Heihei regarded her, then the water. With a little neck bob, he stood up . . . and walked right over the edge of the boat.

"Heihei?" Moana shouted as the rooster splashed down into the sea and began flailing.

"Argh!" she cried just before diving in to rescue the panicking chicken, whose wings were fast getting waterlogged. Of course, that didn't stop Heihei from flapping them in her face, the wet feathers smacking against her cheeks and blocking her view.

Finally, tucking him into a ball with two hands, Moana lifted him up over her head and turned, only to realize that her canoe had drifted away.

Sighing, she tucked Heihei under one arm and kicked toward the boat.

Reaching the hull, Moana half heaved herself up and dumped Heihei over the side. He slipped out of her hand and landed in the bottom of the boat with a thunk.

"Bowk!" he protested.

Moana slid over the side after him and was just getting her legs under her when Heihei strutted toward the edge of the boat. Lunging, Moana caught him and plopped him into the cargo hold.

"Stay," she told him firmly. Heihei's head jerked up and he walked smack into one of the walls, then turned and bonked into another one. "Or that," Moana said. Grabbing hold of the oar, she lowered it into the water. "Okay. Next stop: Maui."

Moana hoisted up the sail, but a huge gust of wind pushed against it, dragging the boat backward.

"Oops," Moana said, quickly tacking to the left so the wind would push her in the right direction. Instead, the boat spun around, facing the way she'd come.

For a brief wistful moment, Moana wondered how much easier it would be if her father had taught her how to sail. But she wasn't one to dwell on what-ifs.

Taking some deep breaths, Moana fiddled with the lines. *Oh, okay,* she thought. *That's the way to do it.*

Several hours later, her arms were starting to tire and she was eying her supplies. After a quick break for a banana and some coconut water, she settled back into her seat.

"I am Moana of Motunui," she rehearsed. "You will board my boat, sail across the sea, and restore the heart of Te Fiti."

Maui would have to listen to her.

As the sun set, a pod of dolphins leapt out of the water then sped away toward the horizon. Where were they headed so quickly? She wished they'd stuck around to keep her company. Heihei was turning out to be more of a nuisance than anything else.

With night came strong winds, and Moana needed all her strength to keep the boat on track as the sail whipped in the gusts. She stole glances at the sky, keeping Maui's constellation in sight, trying to direct the boat toward it.

"I am Moana of Motunui," she recited to herself, the words bolstering her confidence. "You will board my boat, sail across the sea, and restore the heart of Te Fiti."

Finally, the winds rested and a calm fell. Moana breathed a sigh of relief, slumping lower in the bottom of the canoe. That had been rough.

Weariness overtook her and her eyes drifted closed.

• • • • • • • • • • • •

Splash!

Seawater smacked over the hull and into her face. With a sputter, Moana sat up. How long had she been asleep? Rubbing her eyes, she looked up to the twinkling stars.

Where was Maui's fishhook? How had she lost it?

Frantic, she twisted all around, scanning the sky.

There! It was behind her!

Groaning in frustration, Moana heaved on the lines, swinging the boom to turn around. Unfortunately, just at that moment, a blast of wind shoved against the sail, and the boat began to tip precariously.

"No, no, no!" Moana cried, scrabbling to fix it.

Too late.

With an enormous crash, the boat capsized, spilling Moana, her oar, the bags, and Heihei into the sea. Moana churned underwater, then swam up toward the hull, throwing one arm over it.

Gasping, she looked around to see everything from her boat drifting in different directions.

"Uh, ocean, could I please get a little help?" she asked hopefully. If the ocean had entrusted her with the heart of Te Fiti, surely it didn't want her to end up stranded without her supplies.

All around her, the undulating waves sloshed in their same rhythm, ignoring her plea.

Okay, then, Moana thought. *I can do this.* First she retrieved Heihei, dumping him unceremoniously on the overturned hull. Then she dove after her oar, which was drifting away. But by the time she turned her focus to the rest, her supplies were all scattered. Moana struggled after them through the rolling waves. Were the crests getting bigger or was that just her imagination?

BOOM! A rumble of thunder crackled across the sea.

Looking up, Moana saw dark clouds blocking out the stars. *Oh, no, really?* Where had that storm come from? She floundered in the sea, but her supplies were being pulled away from her too quickly. It was no use—she had to abandon them.

Drawing on her reserves of energy, Moana swam back to her boat and tried to lift it.

"Come on, come on," she muttered.

If she didn't get the boat back upright now, she'd have no chance once the storm was fully upon her. But no matter how she shoved, she couldn't leverage the boat back up.

"Help me! *Help!* Please!" she implored the water around her. But whatever magic sometimes curled through the waves to give her a hand didn't respond.

There was nothing for it but to try and ride out the storm. Moana clung to the hull as gale-force winds blew and the sea rose higher and higher to meet them.

Digging her fingers into the wood, Moana squinted her eyes shut and called out to her ancestors as an enormous wave lifted the boat up, up, up . . . and crashed it back down. The next swell was right behind it, slamming her and the canoe with such force that a plank of wood knocked Moana out. *So much for the ocean being my friend,* Moana thought as blackness closed over her.

CHAPTER 9

Something landed on top of Moana, pressing her down into the warm sand. *Sand!* There was sand under her! Shifting her weight, Moana pushed up into daylight.

"*Squawk!*" The something on top of her turned out to be Heihei, who flapped off, stumbling along the beach with a coconut on his head.

Moana's hand flew to her throat. *Phew.* She exhaled as her fingers found the heart of Te Fiti still securely tucked inside her grandmother's shell necklace. For a moment, she'd worried her mission was over.

Now she just needed to figure out where she was. Shaking herself off, Moana stood and gazed around in the daylight, taking in her surroundings. She couldn't see any trees, just low-lying bushes and craggy rocks jutting up like claws, with one tall promontory rising up to the sky. It looked like most of her supplies had washed ashore, along with her boat. Moana frowned as she spotted the canoe, tossed up on the rocks, with who knew what damage from the storm.

"Um." Moana turned and glared at the ocean, gesturing to her boat. "What? I said *help me*, and tidal-waving my boat—*not helping*!"

Tap, tap, tap.

Moana spun at the sound and saw Heihei, coconut still on his head, pecking at a large boulder. Carved into its side were hundreds and hundreds of little fishhooks, all coming together to form one giant fishhook.

"Maui?" she wondered aloud. Could this be where the demigod lived?

She turned back to the ocean, realizing that it had brought her there for a reason. *Oops. Guess I shouldn't have yelled*, Moana thought.

From among the boulders came a clattering of rocks so loud it sounded like a thunderstorm, and a huge shadow loomed up from between two rocks. *Really* huge.

With her nerves zinging, Moana seized her oar in one hand, Heihei in the other, and ducked down behind her boat. She just needed a minute to gather herself. Maui was a demigod, after all.

"Maui, demigod of the wind and sea?" She practiced the words quietly, trying to keep the wobble out of her voice. "I am Moana of Motunui. You will board my boat—no—you *will* board my boat—no—you will *board* my *boat*—yeah! I am Moana of Motunui, you *will* board . . . my . . . " Moana trailed off, glancing around the side of the boat.

His shadow had vanished. Where was he?

"Boat!" a voice boomed.

Oh, wow! He was *right there!* Unable to help herself, Moana let out a little squeak and ducked down.

"The gods have given me a b—*agh!*" Maui had started to lift the boat, but yelped as his eyes landed on Moana, tucked under the outrigger.

He let go, and the boat slammed back down with a thump. Moana rolled out of the way just in time and sprang to her feet. Maui was peering down at the boat and didn't notice as she skirted around him. His broad back—five times her size—was covered in tattoos, and his hair sprung out in wild waves.

Okay, you can do this, Moana thought.

The demigod reached down with one enormous

hand and lifted the boat back up, more tentatively this time. But instead of Moana, he found Heihei sprawled in the sand. The rooster groaned.

"Huh?" Maui said.

"Maui?" Moana asked.

Startled, the demigod swung around, Moana's canoe still in his hand. Moana slid backward to get out of the way as the bow sliced through the air.

Straightening, she planted the pole end of her oar in the ground and propped her other hand on her hip, considering the demigod before her. Tattoos covered his chest and arms, and a string of what looked like teeth was hung around his neck—including a shark's tooth bigger than any Moana had ever seen.

"Maui? Shape-shifter, demigod of the wind and sea?" Moana paused for a deep breath. "I am Moana of Motu—"

"Hero of men," Maui said.

"What?" Moana sputtered, confused.

"'Maui, shape-shifter, demigod of wind and sea, hero of men'—I interrupted. From the top: 'hero of men'—go!" He smiled encouragingly at her like she was a toddler reciting a poem.

"Uh. I am Moa—"

"Sorry, sorry," Maui raised his hands apologetically. "And women. Men *and* women. Both, all, not a guy-girl thing—hero to all!" He leaned down conspiratorially and whispered, "You're doing great!"

What was he talking about?

"Wha—no, I'm here to—" Moana lifted her hands, accidentally waving the oar in the air.

"Of course, yes. Maui always has time for his fans." Maui reached forward and took her oar. With his other hand he plucked Heihei from the sand and used his beak to scrawl something into the wood of the oar. "When you use a bird to write with it's called 'tweeting.'" Maui released Heihei and turned to grin at Moana.

Flabbergasted, she just stared at him as he brandished the oar, now inscribed with a heart and a fishhook. Could he be serious? There were people to help, entire islands to save. And he thought she wanted an autograph?

The demigod raised his eyebrows, then nudged her playfully. "I know, not every day you meet your hero—" he began.

Before he could go off on another confusing ramble, Moana seized one end of the oar and jabbed the other end into Maui's stomach. With a whoosh of breath, Maui doubled over. Moana snatched hold of his ear.

"You are *not* my hero," she snapped. "You are the dirt basket who stole the heart of Te Fiti!" With her free hand she pulled the stone from her necklace and showed it to him. "And you *will* board my boat, sail across the sea, and put it back!"

Tugging on Maui, Moana tried to haul him toward her boat, but he didn't move. What was he made of, stone? Moana gritted her teeth and tried again, yanking with both hands.

Maui arched an eyebrow at her, then straightened to his full height, pulling Moana up off the ground so she dangled from his ear like an earring. Feeling silly, Moana let go and stepped back to glare at him.

"Um, yeah, almost sounded like you don't like me, which is impossible, 'cause everyone knows I only got stuck here trying to get the heart for you mortals," Maui said, brushing off his hands. "So what I believe you were trying to say is . . . thank you."

"Thank you?" Moana repeated incredulously.

"You're welcome," Maui boomed, an enormous grin on his face.

"What? No, that's not—I wasn't," Moana sputtered. Maui was the cause of their problems—she wasn't going to thank him for that!

But Maui ignored her protests. "Yeah, I get it, it's overwhelming when you are in front of someone so cool and powerful." As she watched, one of Maui's tattoos—a picture of himself—began to move, and Maui used one hand to high-five the little Mini Maui.

What? Moana had never seen a tattoo that could move before. This was getting very weird.

"Hey, it's okay, give it some time to sink in—I'm sure it's hard for a mere mortal like you to wrap your head around getting to meet *the* Maui!"

Moana rolled her eyes, but Maui continued, oblivious.

"I mean, think of all the awesome things I've done."

Turning, Maui began walking along the shoreline. His legs were so tall Moana had to run through the sand to keep up. He pointed out his tattoos as he went and the Mini Maui tattoo jumped around, as well, acting out each one of his heroic deeds in the ink. Unlike the real Maui, however, the miniature tattoo version still had his magical fishhook.

"There was the time I raised up the sky, so you wouldn't have to walk around all bent over." As Mini

Maui pushed up some clouds, the humans tattooed on Maui's skin straightened up and cheered.

"Oh, and let's not forget when I brought you fire so you wouldn't freeze at night." Maui tapped on another tattoo, which Mini Maui helpfully leapt over to inhabit. As he handed them fire, a group of tattooed people stopped shivering and clamored to thank him.

"Then there was slowing down the sun"—Mini Maui threw a rope around a fiery circle—"and capturing the winds for you—" The tattoos showed Maui hurling wind into a sail for a group of humans, who jumped up and down to celebrate.

"Not to brag, but there's also the small matter of all the monsters I've slain," Maui continued. A barrage of creatures flew at Mini Maui, one at a time. Swinging his fishhook, Mini Maui beat them all off as Maui nodded along. "Really, I could go on and on. . . ."

Leaning down, Maui jiggled his bicep—as wide around as Moana's entire body—in front of her. The Mini Maui tattoo danced, spinning and whirling and clapping like a one-man band.

Wow, this guy has spent far too much time alone with himself, Moana thought, watching the theatrics of Maui and Mini Maui.

They'd come to the largest rock formation, which jabbed up into the sky like a thumb, and Moana wouldn't have been surprised if Maui had been about to take credit for the land they were standing on right there and then.

"Well, anyway," Maui said, his voice full of false modesty, "I was happy to help. So you're welcome and now you can return the favor!"

Moana opened her mouth to ask what he was talking about, but before she could say a word, Maui picked her up. *Whoa, what is he doing?*

"So, I'll just take that boat and we can call it even!"

Um, NO! Moana thought, squirming in his grip, but he was already lowering her back to the ground.

Laughing, he plopped her down just inside a cave in the rock. Moana just had a glimpse of solid gray walls before Maui rolled a boulder in front of the tunnel, shutting out the light . . . and blocking her inside.

The Story of Maui and the Eel

ne year a dreadful storm pounded the island for days, uprooting trees, flooding fields, and damaging boats as the villagers took cover inside their homes. When the skies finally cleared, the people emerged and began to fix what they could, but much of the harvest was ruined. Hoping for better luck on the lagoon, the fishermen spread their nets but caught little.

Unfortunately, the villagers soon discovered that the storm had brought a giant eel to their waters, as long as four canoes laid bow-to-stern. Whatever fish were left in the lagoon soon fell prey to the ravenous eel. Then the hungry eel turned its beady eyes on the village.

The villagers tried to appease it with gifts of chicken and pigs, but the eel was never satisfied.

"We have nothing left to give, but still the eel demands more," the villagers cried. "It is only a matter of time before it will start to eat us!"

Hearing of their troubles, the great and powerful demigod named Maui flew down from the sky, shedding his hawk feathers for a human form as he landed before them.

"Greetings," he called. "I am Maui, and I have come to rid you of the eel that lurks in your lagoon."

A great sigh of relief echoed through the air, for Maui's strength and agility were legendary and he had slain many a monster in the past. Swinging his fishhook in a few practice strokes, Maui warmed up, cracking his neck.

"Now," he said. "Let us see this eel."

One of the villagers volunteered to take him, and they rowed out together onto the lagoon. The villager pointed out the deep cavern that the eel had laid claim to, but so long was the eel that its entire body would not fit inside. Maui could see the eel's nose poking out and got his first glimpse of how large it would be.

Unafraid, Maui dove into the water and swam straight up to the eel. He cracked it over the nose with his fishhook, waking the eel up.

Its mouth agape in anger, the eel rocketed out of the cavern, its tail lashing so furiously that the water became cloudy with bubbles and it could not see who had attacked it. Maui darted in, punching the eel in the side, but that revealed his location to the eel, who wheeled about, jaws snapping.

Quick as lightning, Maui transformed into a small fish and slipped away, then turned back into a man so he could jab the eel with his powerful hook. Slimy skin wrapped around Maui as the eel's lower half circled around the demigod's waist. Rearing up, the eel fixed its beady eyes on Maui and opened its mouth wide to bite the demigod in half. Maui tried to wriggle free, but the eel held him tight and lunged with its head.

With a mighty push, Maui shoved the coils of the eel up, and the eel bit itself! Recoiling in pain, the eel shuddered and began to flee, but Maui pursued it, driving it toward the beach instead.

As the eel floundered up a river, Maui cornered it and dealt it a fatal blow with his magical fishhook. Grabbing hold of the head, Maui hauled it out of the river as the villagers cheered. Then he dug a deep hole and buried the head, stamping down the dirt on top.

From that spot, the first coconut tree sprouted. And thus, the villagers not only praised Maui for fighting off the treacherous eel, but they also had him to thank for providing them with the most versatile of fruits—the coconut.

CHAPTER 10

"**No, no, no!** *Hey!*" Moana shouted, slamming her hands against the stone. *Ouch, that hurt.* "Let me *out*, you lying, slimy—*Uhhh!*" She screamed in frustration.

She couldn't believe she'd fallen for it—of course Maui the trickster would pull something like this. *Never trust a demigod with an ego complex,* she told herself.

Letting out a warrior's shout, she attacked the boulder, kicking and pounding on it despite the bruises it gave her. When that didn't work, she dug her heels into the rocky floor and shoved against the boulder with all her might. Maui had been able to move it one-handed, but she couldn't even get it to budge. Moana paused to assess her surroundings—maybe she could find a stick to use as leverage.

Wait, was that light coming from the back of the cave? Perhaps there was another way out.

Abandoning the boulder, she tore through the canyon at the back of the cave to where it dead-ended in a pit, open to the sky.

What the . . . ? Moana thought, staring up in surprise at . . . Maui. Except this version was carved of stone.

Evidently the demigod had spent the past thousand years erecting a shrine to himself, complete with an enormous statue.

Moana scanned the sheer rock walls for footholds, but found none low enough, so she clambered up the statue itself. From the top of Maui's head, she began throwing her weight back and forth, slowly rocking the statue off-center.

This was going to work. It had to. And when she caught up with Maui . . .

With a satisfying crash, Maui's stone face smacked into one of the walls and Moana leapt off, flinging her arms and legs out. *Yes!* She'd managed to wedge herself between the two walls in a nearby fissure. Moving first her hands, then her feet, Moana inched her way up until she reached the top of the opening.

Bracing herself with her arms, she swung out of the fissure feetfirst.

"Woo-hoo!" Moana let out a happy yell and did a little dance on top of the rocks. But she couldn't celebrate for long—down below, Maui was sailing off in *her* boat.

Not going to happen, mister, she thought, glaring at him with narrowed eyes. She could hear him singing happily as he hoisted the sail and cut through the waves. Down in the cargo hold, Heihei was pecking the floor of the boat, oblivious to the fact that he and the boat were being taken by a demigod. Moana was willing to bet Maui had brought him along as food, not as a pet. *Don't worry, Heihei, I'm coming.*

If he stayed on his current track, Maui would be passing by the point of the cliff she stood on in just a few seconds. Wasting no time, she raced over to where the rock jutted out into the sea, her feet pushing off almost as soon as they touched down, her arms pumping. At the edge, she launched herself into the air, swooping toward Maui like a hawk diving for a mouse.

Ha-ha! I'm going to catch you! she thought gleefully . . . just before she flopped into the water, yards from the boat.

Splash!

Owww! The front half of Moana tingled in pain, as though the ocean had given her a full-body slap.

Laughing, Maui sailed past her. "I could watch that all day. Okay, enjoy the island," he called. "Maui out!" He waved cheerfully.

"No! Stop! Hey!" Moana shouted, splashing after him. "You have to put back the heart—"

Seawater whooshed into her mouth and she had to stop and tread water as she coughed it out. When she looked back up, Maui was getting farther and farther away.

"Stop! Maui! *Maui!*" She yelled every time she crested a wave, but either the demigod couldn't count strong hearing among his superpowers or, more likely, he didn't care.

Beginning to tire, Moana had to work harder and harder just to stay afloat. Maui seemed impossibly far away and—she glanced back—the island was almost beyond her strength to reach, too.

No, she thought. She had traveled past the reef. She had come all this way. She would not give up yet. She dove forward, her arms hauling her through the choppy water and her legs kicking methodically.

All of a sudden, Moana felt herself getting pulled under the water, but there was no tentacle wrapped around her foot, no teeth around her waist. Instead, an invisible force zoomed her through the sea . . . straight toward her boat!

Fwoomp! The ocean deposited Moana, dripping wet, onto the canoe.

Blinking, she and Maui stared at each other for a beat. What had just happened?

"Did not see that coming," Maui admitted.

Moana didn't have time to analyze the ocean's sudden help. If she was going to get Maui to return the heart, she would have to assert her stance while he was still in shock. Recovering, Moana straightened her spine. "I am Moana of Motunui. This is my canoe and you *will* journey to Te *Fiiiii—*" She ended in a yelp as the demigod casually picked her up and flung her overboard.

As she thrashed in the water, she could see Mini Maui scolding Maui. Not that having a six-inch-tall ink guy on her side would realistically help, especially since Maui didn't seem inclined to listen.

"Get over it," he was saying to his tattoo. "We gotta move."

Now, having the ocean on her side . . . That was a different story.

Fwoomp! The water popped her back onto the bow, Heihei squawking and flapping to get out of the way.

"And she's back," Maui muttered.

Moana pushed the hair out of her face and stood up. "I am Moana of Motunu—*eee!*"

Splash! This time, Maui had plunged the oar into the water and stopped the canoe so suddenly that Moana had fallen right off the front.

Almost instantly, the ocean slapped her back on board. Maui's eyebrows shot up, considering her.

"It was 'Moana,' right?" he asked, his voice flat.

"Yes, and you will restore the heart." She opened her necklace and pulled out the spiral heart of Te Fiti. It winked in the sun.

Snatching it from her, Maui hurled it into the distance as far as he could throw. Moana's eyes widened—she couldn't believe he'd just done that! That was—that was—

Whack! The stone came zipping back and thwacked Maui in the head.

Ha! Maybe that would knock some sense into him. Moana shot him a triumphant look.

Shaking his head, Maui said, "Okay, I'm out." And he dove over the hull.

Fwoomp! A wave pushed him back up onto the canoe as if to say "Not so fast."

"Oh, *come on!*" Maui bellowed, his hands clenched in fists.

"What is your problem?" Moana asked. Why wouldn't he just accept he had to fix the mess he'd started? He had to return the heart. Her eyes fell on the stone, which Maui had twisted away from as soon as he was back on board. *Oh.* "Are you . . . afraid of it?" she asked teasingly, picking it up and dangling it toward him.

Letting out a fake chuckle, Maui backed up until his spine hit the mast. "No, no, I'm not afraid."

Mini Maui popped up to his shoulder and nodded vigorously—*yes, yes, he was!* Maui glared down at him. "Stay out of it or I will put you on my butt," he threatened.

Grinning, Moana held the stone higher, the circle swaying between them.

"Stop it," Maui told her, his voice sharp. "That's not a heart, it's a curse. The second I took it, I got blasted out of the sky and lost my hook. Get it away."

"Get *this* away?" Moana asked, all innocent, the heart of Te Fiti now inches from Maui's nose.

"I am a demigod. I will smite you!" He dodged around her to the bow. "Do you wanna get smote? Smoten? *Agh!*" he cried as she followed him, thrusting the spiral forward. "Listen to me, that thing doesn't create life, it's a homing beacon of death. If you don't put it away, bad things will come for it!"

Moana sat back, considering him. His tone had been deadly serious, all mockery and bravado gone— but she didn't believe him for a second. A homing beacon for death? If anything, it was the opposite— the promise of life being restored to her island. She'd been out on the ocean with it and nothing horrible had happened to her . . . apart from a demigod trying to steal her boat, of course. Her eyes narrowed.

"Come for this? The heart? This heart right here?" She raised her voice and held up the stone, waving her hand from side to side.

As Maui spun his arms, trying to get her to put it down, she grinned—served him right for trying to leave her in a cave.

"Hey, cut it out," he cried, frantic. "You're gonna get us killed!"

"No," Moana said matter-of-factly. "I'm gonna get us to Te Fiti so you can put it back."

Thunk! Narrowly missing both her and Maui as it flew past, a three-pronged spear plunged into the mast, quivering over Heihei's head.

"Bowk?" The rooster pecked at it.

Speechless, Moana followed Maui's gaze over the water to a bank of fog. Through the mist, a dark curved shape began to emerge.

"Kakamora," Maui said, his voice full of dread.

"Kaka-what?" Moana asked. She'd never heard of them.

"Kakamora. Murdering little pirates," Maui explained. His expression was grim as he turned toward her. "Wonder what they're here for," he said pointedly.

Feeling a bit queasy, Moana peered into the fog—the Kakamora's boat looked almost like its own island. She was able to make out a small figure with a very round body perched on top. Wait, was that a coconut? The little person seemed to be a walking coconut. Two more Kakamora popped up next to the first one, identical orbs bobbing up and down as they waved their arms at each other.

"They're . . . kinda . . . cute," Moana said. Why was Maui acting so scared? Was he just messing with her?

Then the Kakamora lifted up their heads—it seemed the coconuts were just body armor—with angry faces painted on them. As they secured their coconut armor in place, they started jumping up and down, shaking their spears. On their grand canoe, drums began to sound, the beats punctuating their war cries like the footsteps of an army.

Moana nervously placed the heart of Te Fiti back inside her necklace. The little monsters were not going to get their hands on it.

Clearing the fog bank, the Kakamora yelped even louder. She could see them loading bunches of spears into what looked like catapults. *Uh-oh.*

"What do we do?" Moana asked. She looked toward the ocean. "Do something! Help us!" she urged.

"Good luck," Maui scoffed. "The ocean doesn't help you. You help yourself."

Moana turned to stare at the demigod, who was already rushing to the back of the canoe.

"Pull the lead, tighten the boom!" he shouted as grabbed up the oar.

Ummm . . . Moana scurried over to the rope lines, her fingers wavering above them. Which one was the lead?

"You can't sail?" Maui asked incredulously.

"I—uh—I'm self-taught," Moana admitted a little huffily. She'd made it this far, hadn't she?

Boom, boom, BOOM! thundered the Kakamora's drums as they approached. Moana's stomach jumped in response.

She whirled on Maui. "Can't you shape-shift or something?" According to his tattooed stories and the tales she'd heard growing up, he could transform at will and defeat any beast. Hadn't he just been bragging about how awesome he was and about all his amazing feats?

"You see my hook?" Maui snapped. "No hook, no powers!"

Okay, then we'll do it without special powers, Moana thought, tugging on a line. *Whoosh!* Down came the sail, crumpling to the boom.

Maui groaned and slammed his hand to his forehead. Moana shot him an apologetic look—she hadn't meant to do that!

Without the wind behind it, the canoe shuddered

to a crawl, the waves gently pushing it wherever they liked.

Thunk! Thunk! Thunk!

Spears thudded into the boat all along the hull and mast, these ones with ropes attached. Heihei pecked at the one nearest him, still convinced it might be food. As Moana watched in horror, the Kakamora began to reel them in, closer and closer to their boat, their drumbeats getting louder and louder. They did not seem so cute now that they were upon them. Peering over the edge, the warriors jeered menacingly, their weapons raised. They might not be as tall as Moana's knees, but there were hordes of them.

And there seemed to be no escape.

The Story of the Kakamora

No one knows where the Kakamora came from, only that one day they appeared on the horizon. At first, their giant canoes were just mysterious vessels that would appear in the distance, popping up without warning and then vanishing just as quickly into the mist that perpetually hung around them.

When voyagers ventured closer, they spotted the Kakamora themselves leaping about and knocking into each other on board their strange curved boats, which were made out of various objects they had found on their travels. Their vessels even grew their own coconut trees—presumably to ensure they always had a healthy stock of the fruit. The creatures were tiny, no taller than chickens, and their bodies were covered completely by coconut shells. The voyagers could only guess at their true forms. But they did not have to guess at the Kakamora's moods—the strange creatures painted faces on their shells and would duck out of sight to swap out expressions as they argued and jostled with one another.

The Kakamora could be seen swiping decorative shells from one another, and sometimes several of them would sneak up on one of their sleeping fellows, startling it awake and jolting it out of a hammock. The hapless victim would bounce and roll along the *deck as the rest hooted and jeered in delight.*

It came to be that men looked forward to Kakamora sightings, enjoying watching the playful antics of the devious creatures. Until the day the Kakamora attacked.

The creatures had cloaked their canoe in such thick mist it wasn't until the boat was right beside them that the men noticed it. Even then, the men did not worry, for they had assumed the Kakamora were unthreatening. But soon the eerie silence from their boat grew unsettling. Usually the Kakamora could be heard drumming or percussing on themselves to communicate.

Curiosity turned to alarm, for as the men watched, the Kakamora canoe suddenly split apart, multiplying again and again into many boats. They formed a ring around the voyagers— trapping them.

Three-pronged spears rained down on the voyagers, disabling their smaller canoe, while drums from within the Kakamora's boats started to pound loudly, shaking the sky. Swarming over the edge, Kakamora warriors catapulted on board the men's canoe.

Despite their small size, the Kakamora were an intimidating sight, armed with vicious spears, their fingernails sharpened to claws. Most terrifying of all, their faces had been painted into gruesome expressions—the mouths twisted or bared in horrifying grimaces. Where their eyes should have been were fathomless dark holes carved into the coconuts.

More and more dropped from above, landing with precision

and surrounding the voyagers. Any lingering amusement at the Kakamora disappeared as the smaller creatures overwhelmed the men with their infinite forces and herded them into the bow with jabs from their wicked spears.

Guarded by the menacing warriors, the voyagers could do nothing as a second wave of Kakamora swept down, ransacking the boat for anything precious and carrying their loot back to their own canoes. When the Kakamora finally left, the voyagers' boat was crippled, their supplies decimated, their treasures taken, and the voyagers deeply shaken by the attack. Barely making it home, they warned others of the dangerous creatures.

Yet no matter how careful future voyagers were, the Kakamora's uncanny ability to sneak up on others resulted in a trail of battered boats and robbed travelers. Group after group returned empty-handed, weary, and stupefied by the fierceness of the tiny Kakamora soldiers.

Beware the fog clinging to the horizon, the drumbeats loud as thunder, the boats that split, the painted faces of horror, the eyes that are empty voids. Beware the Kakamora—for they show no mercy.

CHAPTER 11

Roaring in anger, Maui hoisted the sail then began to yank the spears out of their canoe, hurling them off into the water one by one to get rid of the lines attaching the Kakamora's canoe to theirs. *Good idea,* Moana thought, jumping into action.

As she leaned down to tug a spear from the bow, she glimpsed movement from the Kakamora boat. Looking up, she saw it start to separate—splitting apart into three boats that were spreading out to surround them.

"Their boat is *turning into more boats*!" she cried.

But their problems didn't stop there. Warriors were leaping up onto the ropes and using them to swing over to their canoe!

Frantic, Moana and Maui dislodged the spears as fast as they could. With two hands, Moana yanked the final one from the mast and flung it out over the waves.

"Yup, I just did that." She smiled at Maui. They'd done it!

Bonk!

Two small reddish-pink feet hit her on the head, knocking her to the bottom of the boat. Rolling over with a groan, she saw that there'd been one more spear higher up on the mast with a rope connecting one of the Kakamora's boats to theirs. Now a row of Kakamora was sliding down the rope and dropping down on them, shouting triumphantly. Maui was knocking them off with the oar, but more kept coming.

As Moana jumped to her feet, the heart of Te Fiti hit the wooden planks of the boat with a *thunk*. It must have been knocked loose from her necklace when she fell.

Bouncing merrily, the stone began to roll away, and Moana scrambled after it. The Kakamora warriors spotted it, too, and the chase was on. Moana felt a surge of hope as a wave pushed the boat to the side and the stone slid toward Heihei. Maybe he could stop it. The rooster's head bobbed forward and he plucked the stone from the boards . . . then swallowed it down.

"Heihei!" Moana cried as a Kakamora warrior swooped the rooster up.

The creature drummed a little beat on himself in delight and sprang up onto the mast. Yelping in dismay, Moana lunged upward, but the Kakamora had reached the rope and quickly cut the end from the spear, swinging back toward the main canoe with Heihei in his arms.

Moana could feel herself starting to panic. They had to get it back! Her eyes swung to Maui pleadingly. He had to stop them! "Maui! They took the heart!"

The demigod glanced over, his eyebrows raised. "That is a chicken," he said.

"The heart's in the—we have to get him back!" Moana cried.

Sizing up the fleeing Kakamora and the two other canoes bearing down on them, Maui leapt to the outrigger, pulling the sail taut. Moana clutched the canoe as they leaned precariously to the side.

"Chee-hoo!" Maui shouted. Then, with a sharp tug, he used his weight to pitch-pole the boat end over end, landing with a huge splash and pointing back toward the main Kakamora boat.

Whoa. Moana gazed at Maui in amazement. She had to admit that was pretty cool.

Turning to look out from the bow, Moana spotted

the Kakamora warrior with Heihei being pulled aboard their canoe.

"There!" she called, pointing him out. "Right there!"

Only their canoe veered suddenly to the left. *What?* She spun back to Maui, who was steering them away from the Kakamora.

"What are you doing? The heart!" she shouted.

"They can have it. You got a better one," Maui said calmly, holding up the oar where he'd carved his autograph.

Moana's heart sank. He didn't want to get the heart back. He just wanted to escape.

Well, fine then, she'd do it alone!

Moana snatched the oar from Maui and vaulted toward the Kakamora boat, ignoring Maui's cry of protest.

"Hey, what am I going to steer with? Hey!" he shouted after her.

Whump—Moana's feet thudded down on the Kakamora's boat, which felt as coarse and hairy as a coconut under her toes. Was the whole canoe made out of coconuts?

Climbing higher, Moana reached the next deck

only to find herself face to coconut head with a squadron of Kakamora.

"Coconuts." Moana grinned, a fierce gleam in her eye.

Pounding themselves angrily, the warriors charged toward her, their weapons rattling against their armor. Moana pulled back her oar and then swung it as hard as she could, knocking away the front line. Without pausing, Moana sprang over their fallen bodies, darting through a gap in the crowd. With her eyes fixed on the soldier who was holding Heihei, she zigzagged across the boat, swatting away anyone who came too close.

The warrior was heading for a raised platform where a larger Kakamora stood, a necklace of feathers and teeth around his neck. *That must be the chief,* Moana thought.

Just as the warrior knelt down, holding out the rooster to the chief, Moana bounded up and snatched Heihei from his hands.

Whoosh . . . thunk. A blow dart zipped through the space where she'd just been, hitting the chief instead. He collapsed to the deck and the rest of the Kakamora shook in outrage.

As she raced over to the railing, Moana ducked and wove, blow darts sinking into the wood all around her. Grabbing a rope, she leapt up, kicking out her legs to arc around the mast. The boom swung, bowling over a group of Kakamora, one of whom accidentally sucked his blow dart backward into his mouth.

Moana aimed for a bare spot near the railing, then used the oar to pole-vault herself over the edge toward her boat, which Maui was unsuccessfully trying to pilot using a Kakamora spear.

Looking up, Maui dropped the spear and ducked as Moana and Heihei landed on top of him. Jolted by the movement, the rooster gagged, coughing up the stone into Moana's waiting hand.

"Got it!" Moana told Maui proudly.

The demigod glared at her, then tossed his head to the side. Following his nod, she looked around.

"Oh," Moana said, her excitement fizzling out. The three Kakamora boats were converging on them, their angry warriors shooting blow darts in a barrage so thick, it looked like it was raining.

Unceremoniously dumping her and Heihei to the deck, Maui grabbed the oar from her and stepped over to the sail lines. In a few quick moves, he trimmed the sail and pivoted the canoe to catch a headwind, aiming toward a gap between two of the boats.

Clinging to the bow, Moana could have reached up and brushed the Kakamora's boats as their canoe squeezed past. Once they were through, with nothing between them and the open ocean, she realized she'd been holding her breath and gasped in relief.

Crunch! The Kakamora canoes crashed into one another, the sound an eerie echo of colliding coconuts.

Maui swung their boat into the wind, surging away from the sinking boats. As Moana looked back, she saw the tiny figures of the Kakamora bobbing around in the water, their coconut armor keeping them afloat. They were drumming on themselves loudly and waving their arms, but without canoes, they were no threat.

"Woo-hoo! We did it!" Moana jumped up and down exuberantly.

"'We did it?'" Maui repeated grumpily. "No, *we* didn't do it. *Me* did it. All you did was almost get us killed." He plucked a blow dart from the boom and waved it at her, then began moving down the length of the canoe, pulling out the other darts.

"And get the heart back," Moana pointed out. Neither Maui's grumbling nor the pile of darts he was gathering could pop the bubble of happiness and pride in her chest.

Maui snorted. "You cracked a couple coconuts, hoobeedeedoo!" He turned to face her, his eyebrows drawn together. "You wanna get to Te Fiti, you gotta go through a whole ocean of bad—not to mention Te Kā. The lava monster?" He tapped a tattoo on his skin showing an enormous fiery figure knocking Mini Maui from the sky. "Ever defeat a lava monster?"

"No," Moana said casually. "Have you?"

She arched an eyebrow in challenge and Mini Maui winced and bowed—she'd scored a point there—but Maui just stared at her, his expression not amused.

"I'm not going on a suicide mission with some mortal." Holding up a hand to stave off her interruption, he kept going. "You can't restore the heart without me, and me says no. I'm getting my hook."

The boat creaked as he sat back down and folded his arms across his chest, his lips set in a firm line. Cocking her head, Moana studied him and his tattoos, wondering how she could persuade him. There had to be a way to use his ego for her cause. *Hmmm ...*

"You'd be a hero," she said, sidling up next to him. "That's what you're all about, right?"

Without even glancing at her, Maui lifted a banana from their supplies and began to peel it. "Little girl, I *am* a hero," he said.

"Maybe you were. But now—now you're just the guy who stole the heart of Te Fiti. The guy who cursed the world." She paused, then delivered her final punch. "You're no one's hero."

Seeing her serious expression, Maui's smile faded. He glanced at the water, which seemed to shake its head in agreement with Moana's words.

Moana let the revelation sink in for a few more seconds, then held up the heart. "But . . ." Her voice took on a persuasive tone. "Put the heart back, save the world? You'd be everyone's hero."

Maui's eyes glazed over as though he were imagining the applause, so to help him along, she leaned forward, cheering and clapping next to his ear. Snapping back to reality, Maui swatted her away and shook his head.

"We'd never make it past Te Kā. Not without my hook."

Moana thought about that. There was no denying it would be easier if he had his powers back . . . so they'd make a detour. It couldn't be that hard.

"Then we get it," Moana said confidently. "We get your hook, take out Te Kā, restore the heart. Unless you don't want to be Maui, demigod of the wind and sea, hero to all . . ."

His eyebrows furrowed, Maui considered her plan. Given the excited bouncing that Mini Maui was doing, he was evidently on board. The demigod shoved his tattoo self onto his back so he could make up his own mind.

"We get my hook first," he said.

Moana nodded. "Then save the world. Deal?" She held out her hand.

"Deal." Maui took her hand, then yanked her out of her seat and flung her into the ocean.

She barely had time to sputter to the surface before the waves picked her up and dumped her back on board. Shivering, she glared at Maui.

"Worth a shot," he said, shrugging nonchalantly.

CHAPTER 12

As the sun sank toward the sea, a sprinkling of stars began to appear in the east. Maui lifted his thumb and forefinger up at an angle and sighted along them to one of the twinkling lights. Dipping his other hand in the ocean, he brought it to his mouth as if he was tasting the waves.

What is he doing? Moana wondered. *Can he really tell anything from the* taste *of the water?*

"We go east," Maui announced. "To the lair of Tamatoa. If anyone has my hook, it's that beady-eyed bottom-feeder."

Moana had no idea who Tamatoa was, but she couldn't help bouncing excitedly in her seat. They had a plan! They were off to save the islands—to save Motunui!

Yanking up on a line, Maui raised the sail higher and Moana had to dive to the floor to avoid the boom as it swung sharply over her head. The wind pitched the canoe to the side and Maui leaned his weight back to counterbalance it. He seemed so in tune with the boat, the sea, the wind.

Moana edged closer. This was her chance to watch an expert wayfinder at work. Craning over his shoulder, she mirrored his finger movements as he tied off the sail with a complicated knot, trying to commit them to memory.

Suddenly, Maui turned and, finding her only inches from his face, startled, nearly falling backward.

"Teach me to sail," Moana said, an eager shiver running through her.

"*Wayfind*, Princess," Maui said curtly. "What I do is called wayfinding and it's not just sails and knots; it's seeing where you're going in your mind, knowing where you are by knowing where you've been."

"First, I am not a princess, I am the daughter of the chief—"

Maui shrugged. "Same difference."

"No—" Moana insisted, but Maui cut her off.

"If girls want to wear your dress, you're a princess,"

he said, lifting his hand to wave off any of her objections. "You are not a wayfinder. You will never be a wayfinder."

Picking her up, he set her purposefully in the cargo hold next to Heihei, as though she were nothing more than a pest to be contained. Moana frowned in annoyance and was about to protest when she heard something slap against Maui's backside.

The demigod twisted to see what had hit him, then swung his head to glare at the water around them.

"Really?" he asked. "Blow dart in my butt cheek?"

As Moana watched, Maui crumpled to the deck. His eyebrows scrunched and he frowned menacingly at her. The rest of him was paralyzed, but he could still move his head.

Grinning, Moana clambered out of the cargo hold and used the oar to leverage the demigod up and onto the outrigger.

"You are a bad person," he grumbled as his face smushed against the poles holding the outrigger together.

"If you can talk, you can teach," Moana said cheerfully. She plopped down in the stern and beamed at him, oar in hand. "Wayfinding, lesson one: hit it."

Reluctantly, Maui began to tell her what to do. Thrilled to be learning, Moana didn't even care that Maui's mentoring style was hardly supportive.

"You are literally going backwards," he snorted as she struggled to steer the boat toward the sunset.

Raising her hand, she tried to follow Maui's instructions about how to sight angles.

"You're measuring stars, not giving the sky a high five," Maui said, his tone mocking.

After she dipped her hand in the water, Maui told her: "If the current's warm, you're going the right way."

"It's cold," Moana said. "Wait, it's getting warmer."

Maui started to laugh. Realizing he'd been playing a trick on her, Moana quickly pulled her hand back, shaking it off. "Ew, gross!" she cried.

Still chuckling, Maui told her to untie the halyard.

"Not the halyard," he called out as she tugged the wrong rope loose. She moved over to another one. "Nope. No, no, *no*—" Maui chided her as she hovered over different ones.

Finally at the right one, Moana picked at the knot holding it down, but as soon as the rope was free, the wind whooshed the sailcloth full and the boom swung out over the water, dragging the rope with it.

"Get the rope!" Maui cried.

Lunging, Moana was able to pin down the end of the rope before it went overboard. She pulled it back slowly, hand over hand, fighting the wind with every tug to swing the sail and the boom back over the boat. She was definitely going to get blisters, but she didn't care. Meanwhile, the canoe was rocking more and more. With a swoop, the outrigger was dunked under the water.

Maui sputtered, coughing out water as he resurfaced. "Maybe I could try to teach the chicken."

"Well, your tattoo thinks I'm awesome and he's better-looking," Moana said, winking at Mini Maui. The little guy smiled smugly at Maui.

"Tattoos can be removed," Maui muttered darkly.

With a wicked grin, Mini Maui began waving his arms, drawing the attention of Heihei. Thinking he was some sort of bug, the rooster raced over to the moving tattoo, and Mini Maui darted around Maui's skin, goading Heihei into pecking Maui.

"Not the face! Not the face! *Not the face!*" Maui yelled.

Once the boom was level over the boat, Moana wrapped the rope around one hand to hold it steady and used the other to lever the oar into the water. *Let's see,* she thought. She wanted the boat to go to the left, so she swung the top of the oar that way.

Oops! The canoe skidded to the right, straight into the choppy waves. Moana gritted her teeth. She *would* do this. She thought of her ancestors' boats in the cavern on Motunui. It was in her blood to do this! Quickly, she shifted the oar back the other way and the canoe turned, riding the waves more easily.

Peering at the sky, Moana realized she needed to adjust their course. She gently released the rope slightly and inched the oar to the right. *Yes!*

As the stars shone down on them, Moana strained to keep the canoe at just the right angle, ignoring a spasm in her shoulder and an itch on her ankle. After a while, it became harder and harder to stay awake as her muscles complained and her energy drained away. She shook her head to clear it and repeated her mantra over and over: *I can do it, I can do it, I can do it. . . .*

She would prove it to Maui.

And to herself.

The Story of the Lost Wayfinder

nce a young wayfinder named Laumei set out on his first voyage alone. As he left, his father and mentor watched from the shore, waving farewell. Laumei sailed for two days, exploring the sea, then decided to head home. All was well until he fell asleep at the helm. With a start, Laumei awoke in the late afternoon to find the sky covered in clouds. Laumei had no idea where he had come from or in which direction Motunui lay. All he could see for miles around him was a gray haze, as though the world had been swaddled in blankets.

Deeply ashamed, Laumei hung his head. His father had warned him not to fall asleep while voyaging, and he had done exactly that! What kind of wayfinder was he to have betrayed his training in this way? Perhaps he was not fit to be a wayfinder at all. A wayfinder had to remain awake to know where he had come from and how long he had been sailing so he would know where to go next and how to return home.

Panic built in Laumei's gut and climbed toward his mind, but before it could consume him, he spotted the drum at the center of the boat. Drumming had always helped clear his mind, so he quickly moved to the drum and began to pound.

Louder and louder Laumei drummed, each beat shattering the fear that clutched at him. He was focused, centered. As a wave of calmness washed over him, Laumei remembered who he was: he was a wayfinder. All his years of training cycled through his mind, and an idea came to him.

Lying down, Laumei closed his eyes and felt the rhythms of the ocean pass through the boat. There were the deep, constant pulses of the far waves, flowing from one horizon to the other. Then short staccato waves rapped along the hull, bouncing off from an island. Laumei knew that rhythm. Those were the waves that rippled off Motunui!

Sitting up, Laumei leapt to adjust his oar, steering for home. As he gazed out on the ocean, a tern dove into the sea, then winged back along the path Laumei was taking, proving what Laumei knew in his heart: Motunui was close.

Laumei sailed on, sure of his way and eager to be home with his family. Soon the clouds parted and the sun's rays blazed down, catching on the peaks of Motunui in the distance. The young wayfinder had done it. He'd found his way home and, more important, he'd found the confidence to sail again. Although next time he would be sure to stay awake.

CHAPTER 13

Warm sunlight on her eyelids woke Moana the next day. Stretching, she poked her head up over the hull, an excited thrill running through her at the sight of land ahead. Rising out of the ocean was an island so green and beautiful it had to be Te Fiti.

"We're here? Maui? Told you I could do it!" Moana spun to find Maui asleep at the helm, snoring softly.

Turning back around, she watched the island get closer, the tall cliffs looking familiar. Was that a reef circling the island, as well?

"Motunui . . . But—I'm home?" Moana stared in confusion. It wasn't time to go home yet. They had to restore the heart first.

To her horror, the green mountaintops of her island began to blacken and then, as though rivulets of ink were spilling down over the rocks from above, the plants below withered. Even from the distance, Moana could smell the stench of the rotting plants, the acid tang burning the inside of her nose.

"Moana!" Her father and mother stood on the shore, waving their arms over their heads. Their faces were pained and there was an edge of panic in her father's voice. Behind them, the forest was shriveling so fast it looked like a tidal wave crashing toward the sand.

"Dad? Mom?" Moana cried. She gripped the side of the boat, her heart lurching. She had to help them! She had to save her home!

"Help! Moana! *Moana!*" her mother called.

Gasping, Moana bolted upright, her eyes blinking in the bright daylight. Looking down, she realized her hands were empty—no hull clutched in her palms. No oar or ropes, either.

"Enjoy your beauty rest?" Maui asked mockingly. "A *real* wayfinder never sleeps, so they actually get where they need to go."

Evidently, the demigod had recovered from the dart and had taken over when she'd fallen asleep.

Moana felt a pang of guilt. She was failing her

ancestors. But then again, she hadn't known that rule and it *had* been a long couple of days. Still, she vowed to herself to stay awake next time. At least her nightmare hadn't been real. She sat up, trying to shake off the lingering feeling that something awful was happening back home. She had to believe she still had a chance to save Motunui.

"Muscle up, buttercup. We're here."

Following the direction of his nod, Moana turned to see a ring of fog hovering over the ocean. Bursting through it was a huge rock spire more than a thousand feet tall. When they got closer, Moana had to crane her neck to see the top, but even that disappeared as Maui piloted them through the fog.

Ker-thunk. The bottom of the canoe bumped into the rock-strewn beach at the base of the spire.

As Maui tethered the boat to a rock, Moana wandered closer to the cliffside. In its shadow she found a withered tree—its bark completely black, as though it had been poisoned.

Shivering, Moana fingered her necklace. *That could be Motunui,* she thought, remembering the decaying vines outside the cavern of boats and the horrible images from her dream. But not if she and

Maui restored the heart in time . . . She hoped locating Maui's fishhook wouldn't take long.

"You sure this guy's gonna have your hook?" Moana asked, eyeing the cliff. Who would live at the top of a rock spire that high? Was there anything growing up there, or did he have to come down every day to eat? She couldn't imagine making that climb every day, but then, maybe he could fly.

"Tamatoa? He'll have it. He's a scavenger—collects stuff, thinks it makes him look cool."

Moana turned to see Maui sprinkling some food out for Heihei. *Awww, that's sweet*, she thought. Then the demigod ruined it, pantomiming to the rooster that he should eat up so that then Maui could eat *him*. Stepping in between them, Moana shook her head at Maui: pest or not, her rooster was *not* on the menu. Of course, Heihei cluelessly began pecking at the food.

Maui shrugged, then strode over to examine the cliff face, whistling to himself.

"And he lives . . . up there?" Moana said as she joined him.

"What?" The demigod chuckled in amusement as though she'd made a joke. "Oh, no. That's just the entrance. To Lalotai."

"Lalotai?" Moana felt the blood drain out of her face in shock. Her grandmother had told her stories of that place. "The realm of monsters? We're going to the realm of monsters?"

Maui's tone had been so casual, like it was an everyday thing to venture into a land populated by the biggest, scariest monsters around. Then again, maybe that *was* an everyday thing for him.

"We? No. Me. You're going to stay here . . . with the other chicken." Maui nodded toward Heihei, then grinned at Moana. *"Ba-gock!"* he crowed, flapping his arms. "That's what I'm talking about—gimme some!" He held up his palm to Mini Maui, but the ink guy just stared at him.

Moana's eyes narrowed. She was no coward. Hadn't she already proven herself by voyaging beyond the reef? And in the battle against the Kakamora? No, if it involved Maui and getting the heart back to Te Fiti, she was going to be a part of it, no matter how daunting the task.

"Nothing?" Maui asked his tattoo self. "That was a good one. How do you not get it? I called her a chicken, there's a chicken on the boat—I know she's human, but that's not the—oh, forget it. I'm not explaining it to you. 'Cause then it's not funny!"

Shrugging at Mini Maui, the demigod turned without even glancing at Moana, so her glare was completely wasted, and began to climb up the cliff, his long arms carrying him out of conversational range alarmingly fast.

The spire seemed impossibly high. She hoped the rock wasn't slippery. Casting a glance at the dead tree, Moana reminded herself that her people were counting on her, that the ocean needed her help to stop the spreading darkness. She clutched her necklace and prayed for luck, both from the heart and from her grandmother's spirit.

Then she stepped up onto a boulder, stretching her arms as high as they could go to grab her next handhold, and pushed off with her feet. *I can do it,* she told herself. *Breathe, reach, pull, breathe.*

After about thirty minutes of grueling climbing, she caught up to Maui, who was taking a rest break. When he saw her, he muttered something about idiotic mortals and started upward again, but this time she was able to keep him within sight . . . and within earshot.

"Do you have to breathe so *loudly*?" he complained as she panted below him.

"We can't—all—be—demigods," she gasped out. Then she had to save her breath for climbing, since she was using twice as many hand- and footholds as Maui.

An hour later, Maui paused on a ledge and she drew level with him again. Hauling herself up onto the platform, Moana wobbled slightly then quickly recovered, scanning the rock for her next hold. She could feel his eyes on her as she scrambled up onto a boulder and shook out her hands.

"So . . . 'daughter of the chief,'" Maui began. "I thought you stayed in the village, kissing babies."

Moana shot him a look, wondering where the demigod was going with this line of logic.

"I'm just trying to understand why your people decided to send—how do I phrase this . . ." Maui tapped on his chin. "You?"

"My people didn't send me. The ocean did," she said, reaching up on tiptoes toward the next overhanging ledge.

"Right. The ocean. Makes sense—you're what, eight . . . can't sail—it's the obvious choice." Maui stood and walked over to the boulder, his head at the same height as her waist, although she didn't for a second think he was there to give her a boost.

"It chose me for a reason," she said confidently. Pushing off with her feet, Moana jumped up and wrapped her fingers around the edge.

"That you're expendable?" Maui scaled the cliff to hang next to her. Seeing her annoyance, he chuckled.

"I found *your* island," Moana pointed out proudly. If it weren't for her, he'd still be marooned there.

"The ocean *dumped* you on my island, curly," Maui retorted. He dropped down to the ledge and dusted off his hands. "And if it's so smart, why didn't it just take the heart back to Te Fiti itself? Or bring me my hook? Ocean's a nut job, trust me. BFFs one day, stranding you on a whale-turd sandbar the next!" Maui shouted the last part out at the ocean itself.

Turning back to her, the demigod met her eyes squarely. "Ocean's kooky-dooks," he said simply.

Hundreds of feet below her, the waves crashed against the shore, their movements looking chaotic and frenzied rather than calm and purposeful.

"But I'm sure it's not wrong about you, right?" Maui's voice was mocking and came from right next to her. One of his hands cupped the bottom of her foot and he hoisted her up onto the next ledge in a smooth, effortless move. "You're the chosen one!"

Doubt crept into Moana's mind as she climbed higher. Why *had* the ocean chosen her and not someone older, stronger? Someone who could sail, like her father? The thought of her father—and their last conversation—only made her feel worse. But soon she would help Maui restore the heart and help her people by doing so. All because the ocean believed she was the right person for the job.

Right?

Ahhh! Moana nearly missed a handhold. *Focus,* she told herself. There was no point in worrying about the ocean's choice now. One thing at a time, and the one thing right then was to make it up the spire.

What felt like years later, Moana pulled herself up at the top, collapsing on the rock. But as her heartbeat slowed and she shook out her muscles, her gaze fell on the cerulean seascape before her.

Spread out like an endless tapa cloth around the island, the ocean rippled in every direction for as far as she could see—which, since she was at the top of an insanely high cliff, one that was even higher than the tallest mountain peak on Motunui, was a very, *very* long way. It wasn't just blue; it was aqua and sapphire and navy, emerald and lime green, topped with curling white bubbles and interrupted only by the gray outlines of whales.

The view was so incredible she wasn't sure she'd be able to describe it to anyone back home. Nobody, not even her father, had ever witnessed just how immense and powerful the ocean was beyond their shores. Of everyone in the village, the sea had sought her out.

"The ocean chose you for a reason," she whispered to herself.

"If you start singing, I'm gonna throw up." Maui's voice broke the bubble of serenity in Moana's chest.

Right, they had a monster-land to infiltrate. Turning, she found Maui heaving himself over the edge to join her. Beyond him, all she could see on the summit were jumbles of rocks, rocks, and more rocks.

"So, entrance . . . Not seeing an entrance," she said. Could Maui be wrong about the location?

"Because it only appears after a human sacrifice," he said, his expression ominous.

Moana backpedaled a few steps, eyes darting around in search of an escape route. Was that what he'd meant when he'd said she was expendable?

Then Maui started laughing. "Kidding," he said.

Moana glared at him. "So serious," he teased.

Rolling his eyes at her, Maui shook himself out, then launched into a battle dance, flashing his warrior face.

Crack! His massive fist pounded into the ground and it splintered, the jagged lines forming a face in the rock. Where the mouth would be, a hole opened, and far, *far* below it, Moana saw a spinning vortex appear in the ocean, its center a black fathomless pit.

His eyes full of laughter, Maui nudged her with his elbow. "Don't worry, it's a lot farther down than it looks," he said. Then, with a running leap, he flung himself off the platform toward the water below, shouting: "Cheeee-hoooo!"

Diving gracefully, Maui did a series of flips and somersaults, clearly enjoying himself.

"I'm still falling!" he called up.

As she peered over the edge, Moana felt her stomach roll. Maui's tiny figure disappeared into the swirling maelstrom below, and Moana desperately tried to master her queasiness. For some reason, her muscles weren't listening to her. They seemed to be frozen in place.

"You can do this. Jump," she told herself. Then,

as she saw the portal beginning to shrink, she realized she couldn't wait any longer. *"Go!"* she yelled, jolting her legs into action. Pebbles skittered over the edge alongside her.

"Eeeeeee!" she shrieked as she plummeted toward the vortex. What had she been thinking? All her instincts were screaming at her that she'd just made a terrible mistake, but it was too late. No way to go but down.

The Story of the Lizard from Lalotai

In the depths of Lalotai, the realm of monsters, there lived a gruesome lizard named Pilifeai. As large as a whale, Pilifeai's body was covered in rough, bumpy scales the color of blood, and his teeth were as sharp as obsidian. Even among the inhabitants of Lalotai, Pilifeai was known as vicious, and the other beasts steered clear of him, afraid of his fierce temper.

One day, Pilifeai slipped through a hole into our world. Swimming for days, he reached the reef of a nearby island and clambered up upon the rocks. The bright sun shone down on him and Pilifeai basked in its rays, feeling warm for the first time. When he was hungry, Pilifeai would slip into the lagoon and feast on the fish, then return to his perch on the rocks. If he tired of fish, he swam to the island and hunted through the forest, leaving a swath of broken trees in his wake.

Soon the birds and fish fled the island, scared away by Pilifeai, and the people had trouble catching anything for themselves.

"I will drive away the monster," one warrior declared. Picking up his spear, he climbed into his boat and rowed close to the reef, sneaking up on Pilifeai as he sunned.

Standing up, the warrior balanced carefully in his boat,

then flung his spear with all his might, driving it toward Pilifeai's back. But so thick was the lizard's skin that the spear only bounced off. Awakened from his nap, Pilifeai spun in irritation.

Quickly, the warrior hefted a second spear and threw it toward the lizard's open mouth, hoping it would reach his stomach. But Pilifeai snapped his jaws closed on the spear, breaking it in half. Then, with a swing of his giant tail, Pilifeai smacked the warrior's boat back to shore.

Another brave warrior sailed out, ready for battle. But now Pilifeai was alert and watching for intruders to the territory he had claimed. He dove beneath the water and surfaced under the boat, overturning it.

A third warrior set forth, armed with a bow and arrows. Stopping farther back in the lagoon, he strung an arrow and sighted along its length. Pilifeai watched him from the rocks, his yellow eyes narrowed.

Zing went the arrow through the air, a perfect shot, right to the spot above Pilifeai's eyes. But again, the lizard's thick scales deflected the blow and the arrow slid to the water harmlessly. The warrior launched arrow after arrow, searching for a weak spot in Pilifeai's armored skin, until the lizard grew weary of being badgered so and splashed into the water.

The villagers called a meeting to discuss the matter.

"What can we do?" they cried. "None of our weapons can pierce his skin."

"If earthly tools will not work, let us ask our ancestors for help," suggested a wise elder.

So the villagers gathered in a circle and raised their voices in song, calling upon those who had come before them to return and save their island from the dangerous beast.

The spirits of their ancestors heard their plea and swooped down to the lagoon. As the glowing shapes raced toward Pilifeai, he startled, afraid of their strange light and unearthly speed.

Diving into the deep ocean, Pilifeai swam away, but the spirits pursued him, chasing him all the way back to Lalotai. Then the spirits of the ancestors rode the waves back to the island, where they were greeted by the cheers of the villagers. With Pilifeai gone, the fish and birds returned. But just in case, the spirits remained from then on, patrolling the reef, to protect their people.

CHAPTER 14

The deafening roar of the whirlpool surrounded Moana and she sank into darkness. With a sickening lurch, she saw the last blue of the sky disappear as the hole closed up behind her, and then she was falling through strange, dimly lit waters. Flashes of movement in the periphery of her vision made her turn, but she couldn't see anything. Was she starting to hallucinate as she ran out of air? Or was there another spiraling vortex below her?

Suddenly, Moana passed through what felt like the surface of the ocean, only she was still falling down, not going up. The air around her was odd, like it was charged with lightning, but at least she could breathe—although she was now spinning toward a violet-colored ground that she desperately hoped was soft. . . .

Oof! Instead of hitting sand, Moana crashed into the solid shape of Maui, then bounced off him and began tumbling down a steep bank of tiered levels, almost like the shelves on a coral reef, leading to an eerie glowing forest below.

"Well, she's dead," Maui proclaimed from above her as she careened downhill. That was not encouraging.

"Whoa, whoa, whoa, wh—" Something sticky and gelatinous caught Moana in midair. Well, at least she hadn't landed on her head. A quick look around from her upside-down vantage point showed her a strange world with plants that looked like enormous anemones, pulsing with light from within, and soaring arches of coral everywhere. Poking out in more threatening formations were groups of large, spiny sea urchins dotting the forest.

Everything felt surreal, as though she were on the ocean floor, but she was the size of a shrimp and everything around her was an unnaturally vibrant color. Of course, if she was the shrimp, then that meant she was at the bottom of the food chain. And it seemed Maui had left her there.

All of a sudden, she felt herself being tugged upward. Eyes wide, Moana craned her head to see what was happening.

The sticky substance that had stopped her fall was actually a tongue: a giant pink tongue, which was wrapped around her waist. A tongue that was attached to a bumpy lime-green monster. A tongue that was now reeling her up toward a gaping mouth. She couldn't tell if it was a frog or a lizard that had her in its grasp, but either way, it didn't really matter, since it clearly considered her its next meal.

"Eeee!" Squirming, Moana tried to wriggle free, but whatever the creature was, it was not letting go. *No, no, no,* she thought desperately. Maui was nowhere to be seen, and the ocean—which was beyond the ceiling of the sky far above—couldn't help her down there.

Just as she was about to be pulled into the maw of the beast, something violet streaked across her vision.

Snap! What looked like a purple Venus flytrap lunged down and sealed its carnivorous petals around the frog-lizard monster.

Together, Moana and the tongue—which was still draped around her—dropped toward the ground, the sticky cocoon acting as a cushion to soften her fall.

"Ew! Ew! Ew!" Moana shrugged off the tongue as quickly as possible.

She dove toward the cover of some rocks, not

wanting to become food for anything else. Crouched in a nook, she carefully peered out at the eerie world, wondering where Maui could have gone.

There didn't seem to be any wind, but the anemones waved their arms in an uncanny imitation of trees. Other than that, nothing seemed to stir, but the lack of movement was unsettling. She knew it wasn't empty out there. Adding to the effect were strange plinking sounds that echoed off the coral, making it hard to pinpoint their origin.

Tentatively poking her head out, Moana whispered as loudly as she dared, not wanting to call attention to herself. "Maui? *Maui?*"

Something rustled in the towering kelp beds to her right. Moana's heart relaxed as a silhouette made its way toward her.

"Maui," she said in relief, but the face that pushed through the weeds wasn't his. A lumbering creature that resembled a blowfish with legs emerged, its eyes lighting up when it spotted her.

"Agh!" she screamed, backpedaling frantically. "Maui!"

Fleeing through the anemones, she rounded a curve, the blowfish monster close behind her. The hair on the back of her neck stood up, her senses alerting her she was about to be chomped, when—*whoosh!* A geyser of water burst from a round depression in the ground just behind her, firing the blowfish creature far into the sky.

Moana ducked under an arch of coral, relief coursing through her. That had been close. Taking a few deep breaths, Moana waited until her heart rate was back to normal. Lalotai certainly kept you on your toes.

Whap, whap, whap. Above her, a flock of massive, grotesque bats flapped past and Moana watched their path carefully. She did not want to accidentally walk into their cave later.

As they winged over a ridge, she noticed a curved formation, like a conch shell, stuck on one side. Something glimmered from within it. Drawing closer, Moana peered through a crack in the outer wall and spotted the white sheen of carved bone. Was that . . . yes! It was Maui's fishhook.

Scanning her surroundings, she saw no sign of Maui anywhere. Well, if he wasn't going to come looking for her, she wasn't going to wait for him. She could get the hook without him.

"'I'm a demigod, I have a magicky hook,

hoobidedoo!'" Moana imitated Maui, waving her hands. "I'll get your stupid hook," she said, her voice full of determination.

Circling around to the front, Moana paused outside the entrance. The cave looked dark and forbidding, and a cool wind whistled out of it, carrying the scent of rotting fish.

But if the hook was inside and they needed the hook to defeat Te Kā, then inside was where she would go. She stepped into the darkness, the walls of the cave only dimly reflecting the light from outside. As she walked in deeper and deeper, the path curved around as though she really was inside a conch shell.

From somewhere up ahead came a low light. She was close now. After a few more twists, the passageway opened out into a huge cavern, punctured by several holes in the ceiling to the sky above. There were no monsters in sight. Tamatoa must have been out. But scattered on the floor lay a collection of trinkets: polished pāua shells, jade baubles, decorated spearheads, sparkling gold discs, a net of pearls, and the giant intricately carved white fishhook that she'd spotted from outside.

Moana grinned. She couldn't wait to see the look on Maui's face when she showed up with his hook!

Slowly, she eased forward, placing her feet as carefully as she could to avoid disturbing the treasure and making any unnecessary noise. Surrounded by gems and gleaming metal, she reached the fishhook, an excited spark running through her.

The hook was almost as tall as Moana herself; she'd need to hoist it up onto her back. Bending her knees, she wrapped her arms around the large curve of the hook and lifted, straightening her legs.

But the hook didn't move. Moana slid up its length instead, losing her grip. Frowning, she tried again, then pushed against it with all her might. It still didn't budge. Somehow it was adhered to the cave floor.

Just then, the ground underneath Moana's feet began to vibrate . . . and was it rising? Yes, it definitely was rising in the air, and tilting a bit. A huge serrated claw unfolded from underneath it. Moana's stomach churned with dread. It wasn't the floor she was standing on . . . it was the crab monster Tamatoa's back.

CHAPTER 15

Dropping flat, Moana tried to cling to the crab's shell, using the hook for a handhold, but as Tamatoa spun she lost her grip and slid off . . . right into his waiting claw.

Tamatoa lifted her up, peering at her with his beady obsidian eyes. The blue-and-purple crab was easily fifty feet tall, his front legs tapering into wicked curved points. Sticking up from his shell were all the petrified treasures he'd collected. Treasures, Moana was sure, that the crab protected viciously.

"Yoo-hoo," the crab rumbled, his voice deep and rough, like he rarely used it.

Clutched in his pincer, the jagged edge cutting into her waist, and hanging in midair, Moana heard the scream echoing around the chamber before even realizing it was coming from her.

"Aaaaaaaaarrrgh!"

"Mute that," Tamatoa said, bringing his other claw up to block her mouth. His eyestalks bent lower to examine her, then circled around her. "Human, eh?" he said, watching her look around frantically as the air was forced out of her lungs by his claw. "Pick an eye, babe, it's rude to go back and forth." He flipped her over. "You're a long way from home, or not—I don't know where you live, do I? Except it's probably up there, yeah, not down in the muck with the 'bottom-feeders.' That's what you call us, right? *Bottom-feeders?*"

Fear and shock were distracting Moana from Tamatoa's words. What was he talking about? Was he really concerned about what people thought of him? Thinking back, Moana realized Maui *had* referred to him as a bottom-feeder. . . .

"Well, not with this shell, baby!" Tamatoa shouted, baring his teeth in a yellow smile and pointing with his claw to his back. "Do you see all my sparkly treasures? All my glittery baubles? No one can call *me* a plain Jane." One of Tamatoa's eyestalks pivoted to admire his own shell, which was crammed with bright jewels and precious possessions. "Oh, you may have heard it's what's on the inside that counts, but don't believe it. Outer beauty brings real happiness."

Despite all the shiny trinkets adhered to his shell, Tamatoa was clearly insecure. Moana tried to shake her head, but his claw was clutching her so tightly any movement hurt.

"Not convinced, are you?" Tamatoa's eyes peered at her and the crab looked annoyed. "But *you* were drawn to my shiny collection, weren't you? You see? Point proven. And yeah, that's a bit of an added bonus," Tamatoa continued, lifting her higher. "There are plenty of little parasites like you that are attracted by my sparkly shell. Dinner comes to me!"

"No!" Moana shouted as Tamatoa flipped her up into the air, his mouth opening wide to catch her. This couldn't be happening. She had gone beyond the reef and found Maui and escaped the Kakamora and even started to learn how to wayfind. How was she about to be crab food after all that?

As she spun upside down, Moana saw Maui on top of Tamatoa's shell. Yanking his hook loose, Maui leapt up, wrapping one arm around her and holding her aloft as they fell to the floor so that his legs absorbed the impact.

Setting her on the rocky floor, he shot her a quick smirk. Moana blinked up at him, speechless, as he hefted his magical fishhook, twirling it in one hand before smacking the flat side down into his other palm. "I'll take it from here," he said, his voice brimming with confidence. "It's Maui time." With a glint in his eye, he turned to his tattoo self and asked: "Whattya say, little buddy?"

Mini Maui shifted, his ink re-forming into the shape of a hawk, its claws outstretched as though ready to pounce.

"Giant hawk? Coming up!" Brandishing his hook at the crab, Maui let out a warrior yell. "CHEEE-HOOO!"

As Maui raised the hook above his head, it began to glow brighter and brighter with a brilliant yellow light. Tamatoa scuttled backward, his claws raised to shield his eyes.

Moana's face lit up in amazement as the hook's power flowed over Maui's skin and he began to morph. He was shape-shifting!

Silver scales gleamed and then a large . . . fish . . . flopped to the cave floor.

Moana blinked in confusion. Hadn't he been

planning on turning into a hawk? The fish squirmed, then zapped into a green bug, its wings whizzing rapidly as it buzzed off the stone. As she peered at the bug, it ballooned in midair and crashed down to land on four hooves. Staring up at her was a spotted pig, its face crinkled cutely in puzzlement, reminding Moana a bit of Pua. Shaking itself from snout to tail, it poofed back into Maui.

The demigod tapped his fishhook, his eyebrows furrowed. "Chee-hoo! Chee—" He glanced up at Moana apologetically. "This never happens to me. Chee-hoo. Come on . . ." he muttered, shaking the hook harder, as though the magic just needed to be rattled loose.

Thunk! An enormous blue leg punched into the ground next to them, making Moana jump. Moana and Maui looked up to find the giant crab looming over them again, a sinister smirk on his face.

"Missing your *mana*, hmmm?" Tamatoa rumbled. "How embarrassing for you. Guess you're not as powerful as you used to be."

With one mighty swing, Tamatoa knocked Maui into the air. The demigod flew across the cavern, smacking into the wall with a hideous thud before sliding to the floor.

Stunned, Moana felt a surge of relief when Maui staggered to his feet, clearly injured but conscious. Although perhaps not for long. Tamatoa charged over, claws outstretched. The enormous crab lashed out at Maui in a series of powerful blows, flinging him from side to side.

"Stop it!" Moana cried. Picking up a rock from the floor, she pitched it at the crab. Years of knocking fruit loose with stones had given Moana excellent aim, but even though she hit him square in the back of an eyestalk, Tamatoa ignored her. She bent for another stone.

Before she could stand up, Tamatoa plucked her off the ground in his pincers and dropped her atop a pile of bones, the curved skeletons forming a wall around her.

Straight in front of her, she spotted a crack in the cavern wall, the greenish hue of the sky shining through it. The fissure was small, but she could squeeze in and Tamatoa wouldn't be able to follow her. Only . . .

Moana glanced back. Tamatoa had Maui trapped—the jagged point of a leg pinning the demigod to the floor. As she watched, the crab plucked up the fishhook, turning it over and over.

"The great Maui . . . Without your hook—not so great." Tamatoa clicked the hook back in place among his collection. Maui struggled, trying to lift his head. "Admiring the shell? You know, in some ways, it was inspired by all your tattoos. I just happen to like my artwork, well, *shinier*. Too bad yours can't help you now."

Pushing his claw into Maui's back, Tamatoa pierced a tattoo Moana had never noticed, since it was usually hidden by Maui's hair.

It showed a woman and a baby, and while Moana had no idea what great feat it depicted, it was obvious that Tamatoa pressing on it was agonizing for Maui. He grimaced in pain and wriggled, trying to break free.

"You're always trying so hard to be loved, but no matter what you do for the humans, it will never be enough to fill that void inside you. Don't you know the secret, old friend? You really have to start by loving *yourself*, Maui. And for that, you really have to be beautiful, I hate to say."

Casually, Tamatoa let Maui up, then swiped his claw against him, sending Maui crashing against the wall.

"Just like me. I love every shiny thing about myself," Tamatoa gloated as he picked Maui up. The demigod's eyes bulged as his chest was squeezed.

That did it. Moana leapt to her feet and wriggled out between the ribs of a fish skeleton, a plan in her head.

"I have something shiny!" she shouted, holding up the spiral-engraved stone.

Tamatoa's jaw dropped as he spotted her treasure.

"The heart of Te Fiti," he said, his voice awestruck. Dropping Maui unceremoniously, he pounded across the cavern, his claws twitching as though they were itching to cradle the stone. The entire floor trembled from the force of the crab's charge, and Moana slipped on the shifting surface.

As she tumbled to the ground, the circular stone she held went flying—bouncing and rolling along the floor straight toward a deep crevice. Everyone seemed to inhale as the stone wavered on the edge . . . before dropping into the darkness.

CHAPTER 16

Roaring, Tamatoa lunged for the crevice. It was closer to Moana, but instead of racing him to it or even taking the opportunity to help Maui, she bolted toward the giant crab. With a flying leap, she landed on one of his legs and scaled it to clamber up onto his back. Tamatoa was so fixated on getting the heart that he didn't notice or care.

Quickly, Moana dislodged the fishhook and slid back down to the floor, the weight of the hook pulling her to the ground like an anchor. Using two hands, she lugged it over to Maui, who gazed at her in disbelief, shock freezing him in place.

"You okay?" Moana asked him, her eyes darting to the cut on his back over the tattoo of the woman and baby.

Still somewhat stunned, Maui merely nodded. He reached up to rearrange his hair to cover the tattoo, his face puzzled.

Gripping his arm, Moana tugged him toward the crack she'd seen earlier. "We gotta go," she urged.

"But—the heart—" Maui objected, his expression torn.

"He can have it," she said casually, pulling her necklace from her top. "I've got a better one."

The true heart of Te Fiti winked in the light, and Moana grinned up at Maui's impressed face. She could teach him some tricks, too.

Just then, Tamatoa let out an angry bellow, having found the ordinary rock Moana had switched with the heart before rolling it into the crevice. Claws clenched in rage, he whirled toward them, his obsidian eyes full of malevolence and his teeth clacking angrily as he reared up to his full height.

Uh-oh, thought Moana. "Come on, run!" She began shoving at Maui to get him moving.

Tamatoa charged toward them, his face livid. At the last second, Moana pushed Maui forward and dove to follow him. *Crack! Boom!* Tamatoa rammed into the cavern wall and kept right on going—the momentum of his attack carrying him straight through the wall and out onto the hillside.

Waving at Maui to follow her, Moana burst through the hole Tamatoa had just created for them. As they emerged from the lair, a green glow suffused Maui and he suddenly popped into the shape of a fish again. Moana scooped him up and skidded down the sandy hill, right between the giant crab's legs.

Spotting a geyser, Moana raced over to it, but when Maui transformed back into a human, he grew much too heavy and she was forced to drop him, giving Tamatoa a chance to catch up.

Gnashing his mandibles, Tamatoa stampeded after them. Just as the crab reared up to attack, Moana hauled Maui into the circular dip and then the water spout erupted, launching both of them high in the air to the ceiling of water above.

As they flew through the sky, she looked down. The force of the geyser had knocked Tamatoa over and the crab crashed to the ground upside down, his treasures cracking free of his shell and scattering in a wide circle around him.

Almost immediately, the monsters of the deep swarmed, Tamatoa's collection the most tempting prizes in Lalotai.

"No! That's mine!" Tamatoa screamed as the monsters swept up the trinkets. "Stop it!" But trapped on his back, his legs waving helplessly in the air, the enormous crab could do nothing to stop them.

Once the ground around him had been picked clean and the crab was left treasure-less and alone, he waved his legs pitifully. "Little help," he called. Nobody answered.

Up, up, up, Moana and Maui shot straight through the ocean and burst out into their sky, before crashing down into the water near the spire island.

Now that they were safely back in their world, Moana did a little victory dance in the shallows. "Whoo! We're alive, we're all—*aaagh!*"

Turning, she found herself face-to-face with a shark. She let out a strangled cry before realizing it was Maui. He had the head of a shark, but the rest of him was in human form.

"Listen," the shark rumbled. "I appreciate what you did down there, it took guts, but, uh—"

"Mm-hmmm, mm-hm, mm-hm . . ." Moana nodded at him, taking a few subtle steps back to put some distance between herself and the disturbing sight of a semi-transformed Maui.

"Sorry, I'm trying to be sincere for once, and it feels like you're distracted," Maui said. Wearing a frown, the shark's mouth was even more intimidating, the wall of sharp teeth glinting ominously.

"No. Nope." Moana widened her eyes, trying to look focused.

"Is it because I have a shark head?" Maui asked.

Moana pretended to peer at him. "Do you have a shark head? Because I didn't even—"

"You know what, then don't look at me," Maui huffed, twisting to face the sea.

"Well, I can't *unsee* it, and you smell super fishy," Moana admitted.

The shark's eyes rolled. "The point is, for a little girl—*child*—who had no business down there, you did me a solid."

Moana smiled in satisfaction. It must be hard for Maui to acknowledge getting help from a mortal.

"But," Maui continued, his tone serious, "you also almost died and I couldn't even beat that dumb crab, so chances of beating Te Kā? Bubkes. This mission is cursed." Shaking his head side to side, Maui ran a hand along his fishhook.

"It's not cursed," Moana insisted. He really needed

to change his attitude. They'd gotten that far, hadn't they?

Maui lifted his hand and pointed at his skull. "Shark head," he summarized.

"It is *not* cursed—you're just rusty. We'll practice on the boat." With a little nod of determination, she turned toward where they'd moored the boat, but all she saw were waves. "Where's the boat?"

Sloshing over to where it had been tied up, she found the tattered end of the rope lying on the rocks, a few specks of pebbles around it. Heihei must have mistaken the gravel for birdseed and pecked at the rope till it freed the boat. Moana's heart dropped. The adrenaline she had felt from escaping Tamatoa's lair now turned into frustration. How in the world were they going to find Te Fiti without a boat?

"Cursed," Maui repeated unhelpfully, the fishy stink of his breath coming from right behind her as he peered over her shoulder.

Moana felt the blood rush to her head, her body trembling in anger. Clearly, *he* wasn't going to figure out a solution. *Right,* she thought. *Every problem has its solution. What is the solution?* But Moana's mind started to swim, replaying the vision of Heihei pecking at the rope over and over.

"Could you—if you could—just one sec—I'm just gonna—" Wading up onto the shore, Moana stomped off behind some boulders and began kicking at the sand. How the heck had Heihei managed to lose their boat—not to mention himself with it? "Stupid chicken!" she shouted, hurling rocks at the spire. She couldn't believe it! Well, yes, she could believe it; Heihei pecked at the most ridiculous things, but really? This was the last thing she needed. What were they supposed to do now? Stay on this stupid island forever?

Sinking to her knees, Moana felt defeat lower over her shoulders like a blanket. But as she stared at the rock wall in front of her, her eyes landed on a blackened vine. She peered over at the other side of the wall and gasped. In their haste to get to Lalotai she hadn't noticed the grim scene in front of her. The island was a wasteland with not a speck of green in sight—just the gnarled remnants of trees and bushes. Everything was dead—black and dry—already decimated by the darkness that was spreading across the ocean. It was just like her dream.

And if she didn't do something, Motunui would

soon be as barren and lifeless as this rock spire.

Moana took a few deep breaths, calming herself down. Nobody had said it would be an easy mission, but her people needed her. She couldn't give up now. Shaking the sand off her skirt, she stood and returned to the shoreline, where shark-headed Maui was sitting slumped on the beach, staring at his fishhook, which lay on the sand a few feet away.

Moana stopped in front of him and waited until he looked up at her. "My island is dying," she said. "And I was sent to get you to Te Fiti to restore the heart. My people, my family—"

Maui cut her off, his tone consoling but firm. "We have no boat."

An odd pounding noise came from the sea. Moana and Maui turned together to find that the broken remnants of one of the Kakamora's boats was drifting their way. Three Kakamora sat on board, playing some kind of game with rocks, percussing on themselves every once in a while.

Spotting Moana on the shore, the Kakamora wobbled in alarm and painted new worried faces on their coconut heads. They clearly didn't want to confront her again. As one, they rushed to the edge of their makeshift boat and dove off into the water, their pink legs kicking furiously to carry them in the opposite direction.

Well, wasn't that lucky? Moana smiled down at Maui, whose eyes were narrowed skeptically.

Holding up her hands, she forestalled his objections. "Before you say 'we can't sail that to Te Fiti,' we don't have to. We only have to get to *my* boat, which we will then sail across the sea to restore the heart of Te Fiti," she said.

"You are forgetting a lava monster," Maui muttered.

"You'll beat Te Kā."

"Because you said so." Maui crossed his arms and stared at her, his eyebrows drawn down in disbelief.

"Because you are Maui," she answered. Grabbing hold of his hook, she struggled to pull it toward him. It was heavier than it looked. Maui shook his head, but she didn't let up. "*You* are the *great Maui.* Shape-shifter. Demigod of the wind and sea. Hero of men!" She paused, shoving the hook toward him.

As Maui reached out and grabbed it, he morphed into a shiny beetle.

"—and women," Maui chirped, his bug's voice higher than normal.

Moana couldn't help smiling. "Not yet," she told him teasingly.

Transforming back into his human shape, Maui shot her an answering grin. He strode down to the water and waded in, dipping his hand into the waves.

"Swell's coming from the deep—wind's out of the west, and the chicken's got a big head start," he said, his head cocked as though the ocean were talking to him.

"Great." Moana joined him in the shallows. "Then you have plenty of time to practice."

CHAPTER 17

Once they were aboard the Kakamora's boat and out on the open water, Maui set their course to find Moana's canoe. As if eager to help them on their way, the clouds cleared from the sky and the current seemed to flow faster.

After quenching her thirst with a coconut, Moana took over steering so Maui could have his hands free.

"Why don't we try out some shape-shifting?" she said. "Mini Maui can pick a shape and then you turn into it."

"All right, let's do it!" Maui pumped his arms up and down. He cracked his neck and assumed a wide stance.

Mini Maui copied his warm-ups, then swirled, his ink re-forming into a shark. That was smart—

since Maui had already partly transformed into one recently, maybe it would be an easier one for him to handle and give him some confidence.

Maui clutched his fishhook and concentrated until both he and the hook began to glow. *Pop!* A sardine flipped through the air where the demigod had been.

"Try again," Moana said hopefully. At least he'd completely transformed that time.

Gripping the hook, Maui glowed brighter . . . brighter . . . and *pop!* Ta-da! Balancing on the boards was a shark, grinning triumphantly—until—*pop!* With an abrupt burst of light, the shark was replaced by an enormous blue whale.

Sploosh! Overwhelmed by the weight and size of the whale, the already shabby boat sank under the water.

Hmmm. Maybe we should try another angle, Moana thought, treading water as a sheepish Maui—back in demigod form—lifted the boat out of the waves and tipped it to empty out all the water. Setting it back down, he climbed aboard and hauled Moana up, as well.

Maui gritted his teeth, a shark's fin emerging from his back. First one, then the other of his arms turned into fins. It was working! Except then the fins began to shrink until, all at once, a shiny beetle scuttled along the planks where Maui had been.

Moana grimaced. This was not going well. "Maybe we should try something else instead," she suggested. "How about target practice?"

Tying off the sail line and using an oar to keep the boat on course, Moana hefted one of the coconuts the Kakamora had left behind. Whacking coconuts always made *her* feel better. "Bet I can hit your head," she taunted.

Never one to refuse a challenge, Maui puffed up his chest and gripped his fishhook. "Bring it on."

Winding up, Moana pitched the coconut at Maui's forehead. It whistled through the air, Maui swung the hook, and . . . *bonk!* Maui's timing was off and he missed the coconut completely . . . well, except with his head. Moana winced sympathetically.

"Ouch." The demigod rubbed his head, then shook his muscles loose and resumed his batting stance.

Thwack! The fishhook grazed the second coconut but flew out of Maui's hands into the water.

Thunk! On his next swing, Maui sank the fishhook

into the deck, which vibrated so hard from the impact that Moana fell over.

Maui continued to miss coconut after coconut, most of them ending up in the ocean, but Moana only decided they needed a break when his fingers slipped and he dropped the hook on his own head.

"Great," he said flatly.

· · · · · · · · · · · · ·

As the day wore on, Maui continued to struggle with both shape-shifting (bird with crab's legs; goat instead of pig; turtle with shell upside down) and hook-wielding (a few more capsizes from all the running and jumping).

Soon the sun began to set, filling the sky with sweet pinks and brilliant oranges, illuminating everything with a beautiful glow. Maui tried to become a hawk, one of his favorite shapes. Yet again, he messed up, transforming into a worm instead. Maui popped back into human form and flung the hook down into the hull with a grunt of frustration.

"It's not happening," he grumbled, flopping to lie flat on the floor. "We're doomed."

Moana couldn't let him get discouraged. She knew

it was hard to keep going when you felt lost, but if he kept trying he'd get it eventually. She couldn't let him wallow in self-pity. What was it her grandmother had always said? Self-pity was a bottomless pit—and very hard to climb out of once you fell into it.

"Just stop," she said.

"Doomed, doomed, doomed!" Maui cried dramatically.

Moana leaned forward, poking him with the oar. "Break time's over. Get up."

"Why? You got another speech? Tell me I can do it 'cause 'I'm Maui'?"

Mini Maui clambered up onto Maui's shoulder and waved his arms at him, gesturing that he should stand up and try again.

"Take a hike," Maui snapped, twisting up on his elbow so he could shove Mini Maui to his back.

As the little ink guy slipped down Maui's shoulder blades, the tattoo of the woman and the baby caught Moana's attention. Tamatoa had seemed to target that image . . . but why? What was its story? Maybe if she could remind Maui of all the wonderful things he'd done, he'd remember who he was and feel ready to try transforming again.

"How do you get your tattoos?" Moana asked.

"They show up when I earn them," Maui explained.

"How'd you earn that one? That Tamatoa was poking at? With the lady. What's that for?" Moana leaned forward, tugging his hair aside to see it.

"Mmm?" Maui peered over his shoulder at the woman with the long, flowing hair inked on his skin. Quickly, he rolled onto his back and shifted away so she couldn't reach him. "That tattoo is man's discovery of Nunya."

"What's Nunya?"

"Nunya business," Maui said, waving his hand dismissively.

Rolling her eyes, Moana nudged her oar against him. "I'll just keep asking. What's it for?"

Maui ignored her, so she gave him another poke with the oar.

"You need to stop doing that," he said flatly.

"How'd you get the tattoo?" she asked again.

"Back off," Maui snapped.

Undaunted, Moana tapped him again. "Tell me what it is."

"I said back off."

"Is it why your hook's not working?"

Maui's lips pressed into a thin line, but he didn't answer, even after she whacked him again.

The sun had fully set now, the night sky greeting them like an old friend with its midnight-blue color and twinkling stars.

"Maui, whatever it is, you have to tell—"

As Moana brought her oar around to thwack him, Maui blocked it with his fishhook. *Thunk*. Spinning, Maui flung Moana off the boat, and she landed hard in the dark water.

Spluttering to the surface, Moana stared at Maui in surprise. The demigod looked somewhat embarrassed by what he'd done, but he was clearly still also mad at her. He crossed to the other side of the Kakamora's boat and sat down facing away from her.

This was more serious than she'd thought. Maybe it *was* the reason his magic was defunct. Moana heaved herself out of the water and studied him, a frown creasing her face. Whatever had happened, thinking about it still brought him pain. But how could she help him if she didn't know what the problem was? She couldn't *make* him open up. She lifted her arms in frustration.

"You don't wanna talk, don't talk. You wanna

throw me off the boat, throw me off. You wanna . . . you wanna tell me I don't know what I'm doing . . . I know I don't." She paused, feeling how true that was. She had no clue how to do any of this. The ocean hadn't handed her a map with step-by-step instructions for restoring the heart of Te Fiti. "I have no idea why the ocean chose me. You're right. But I came anyway. My people don't even go past the reef, but I am here—for you." She thought about how far she'd come. She hadn't let any of the obstacles along the way stop her, but now . . . now she was stuck. "I want to help," she said softly. "But I can't if you don't let me."

For several moments the only sound was that of the water brushing along the side of the canoe. Maui's shoulders were slumped and he gave no indication he'd heard a word she'd said. Maybe he needed some time. Moana had begun to turn away when Maui's voice stopped her.

"I wasn't born a demigod," he said, his eyes still fixed on the water.

Moana spun to face him and he half twisted so she could see his profile.

"I was born human," he continued. "I had human parents. They, uh—" He smiled, but it didn't reach his eyes. "They did not want me. They—they threw me into the sea. Like I was nothing."

Looking at the tattoo again, Moana realized the long-haired woman must be Maui's mother. The small figure dropping from her hands was Maui as a baby. Her heart twisted. What a terrible feeling that must have been. To know his own parents had abandoned him. Even though she and her father had disagreed about the ocean, she couldn't imagine what it would have been like to grow up without the love and support of her family.

"I only lived because of the gods. And they gave me this." He lifted up the hook. "*They* made me Maui. And back to the humans I went. They asked for help: 'We need islands! Fire! And coconuts!' It was never enough, though."

As his voice grew wistful, something clicked for Moana. All the dangerous, risky feats Maui had done, all the tricks and stunts he'd pulled—he'd been trying to impress the humans, to make them love him the way his family never had.

"That's why you took the heart. Why you do all of it," Moana said softly.

Maui finally looked at her, his face vulnerable.

Then he cast his eyes down again, threading his fingers together as he waited for her reaction.

Moana looked up to the sky, then out at the sea, where the reflection of the stars danced in the waves.

"You are not nothing," Moana said firmly. "And maybe the whole reason the ocean sent me here is to help you see that."

Maui cast a sideways glance at her, then went back to studying his fingers, but Moana could see her words sinking in and the demigod starting to perk up.

The waves lapped against the hull in a soothing lullaby, and the full moon shone down brightly as he reached for his hook and pulled it closer.

"Pretty good speech." Maui's voice was carefully flat and he peered down at his hook to avoid her gaze, so Moana knew he was touched.

As she watched, Mini Maui reached out his arms and seemed to embrace Maui's bicep. Maui smiled down at him and wrapped one hand around the little guy to hug him back.

After a moment, Maui coughed and patted Mini Maui on the back. "Okay, now it's weird. Let's get to work," he said.

Lifting his hook, Maui swiped it through the air, the

wind whistling as the hook spun. With a grin, Moana set her stance and swung the oar at him. *Thunk*—Maui blocked it with his hook, then countered with a strike of his own. Raising the oar, Moana blocked it. Grinning, the two of them sparred, their feet tapping back and forth across the boat.

From then on, Maui and the hook seemed more connected—the shapes he chose getting clearer and the changes coming faster and faster. Whirling the hook through the air, he demolished target after target, drenching the boat in coconut water.

Next Moana had him shape-shift between swings—going from a human to a shark, thwacking the coconut with his tail, then to a hawk to dive away from the next one. They worked all through the night. As morning dawned and they passed an island, Maui soared up in hawk form, then somersaulted into human form and split a cliff down the middle with his hook.

Moana cheered wildly as Maui the hawk coasted down to the deck then shifted back into human form, smiling from ear to ear.

"You're ready!" she cried.

He held out his hand for Moana to fist-bump, but her eyes widened in excitement as, over his shoulder, she saw a familiar sight in the distance. It was her canoe drifting on the waves ahead. On board, Heihei's head popped up, glanced around, and disappeared again. *Stupid chicken,* Moana thought happily.

Maui followed her gaze and they shared a grin. As they watched, the canoe suddenly lurched and began zooming in their direction. Was the ocean helping them again? No, there seemed to be something large under the surface. Whatever it was, one of the ropes had snagged on it and now the boat was riding almost on top of it. Wait, was that a—

"Giant eel—Maui, giant eel. *Giant eel!*" Moana prodded him repeatedly in the arm. This was the ultimate test to make sure his powers worked!

A sinister gleam lit Maui's eyes and the hook glowed in his hands.

• • • • • • • • • • • •

"Eel's pretty good," Maui commented later as he chomped on a bite of meat—their dinner.

They had done it. Moana had expertly guided their rundown vessel to the eel—and their boat—and Maui had slain the monster with his magical fishhook.

They had made a great team, a fact that was not lost on Moana. It had been a good day.

Moana kicked her feet in the water from the edge of her canoe and pulled back a stick she'd been using to roast a section of eel over the burning remnants of the Kakamora's boat. The sun was setting once more, disappearing from the horizon, leaving room in the sky for the moon.

"Yeah, tastes like chicken," she said.

Feathers brushed her elbow as Heihei teetered forward. *Oops,* she thought. But the rooster just stared at her blankly, then flapped up to the edge of the hull and stepped off. Before she could reach out and rescue him, the water rose up and deposited the drenched chicken back in the hull.

Moana finished her dinner and stood, happy to be back on her boat. She noticed Maui was now standing by the oar, holding a hand up to the sky. She followed suit, peering up at the stars through her fingers, trying to see what he was seeing. Maui turned and, to her surprise, lifted her arm higher, placing it at just the right sighting angle.

"Next stop Te Fiti?" he asked, handing her the oar.

Moana gaped at him. Was he really going to let her

navigate? Was he going to teach her how?

As if in answer to her silent questions, Maui gave a slight nod.

Moana grinned widely, taking the oar from him. "Next stop Te Fiti."

She took her position as the moon rose higher into the sky, shining brightly and bouncing off the gentle waves.

"Lesson one: spot the stars, feel the swell. The sky and the sea are talking to you. Find your way," Maui told Moana. He took a step back.

"That's like three lessons," Moana said dryly.

"I'm a demigod of the wind and sea, not math," Maui replied with a shrug.

He lay down in the boat, leaning his weight so that Moana's hand lined up with the guiding stars they needed.

Moana placed the oar into the water, grateful to Maui for giving her the tools to set a path. She tightened the sail, letting the wind carry them across the ocean and through the night.

A patch of clouds drifted past the moon, diffusing its light into an arc across the sky. Gramma Tala had always said moonbows like that were good luck, and it seemed she was right. Moana smiled at the thought of her grandmother watching over her now. *I'm doing it, Gramma,* Moana thought. *I've found my purpose. And it is wonderful.*

The Story of Maui Lifting the Sky

 housands of years ago, when the world was still young, the sky used to hang low over the ground. To get anywhere, people had to walk stooped over, their backs bent. One day, Maui, great demigod of the wind and sea, was resting near a well, when he saw a woman pass by, doubled over and dragging her water bucket behind her. With each step, water sloshed over the edge because she could not hold the bucket level as she pulled it along.

This is terrible, *thought Maui.* She cannot stand up to carry her bucket because the sky is too close to the earth.

Looking around, Maui saw that all the people were likewise constrained by the lowness of the sky. If they could stand upright, *he thought,* they could do so much more and their backs would not ache.

Determined to help them, Maui walked up the hill to where the sky brushed the grass.

Maui lay down parallel to the sky. He lifted his fishhook with one arm and made a fist with the other. He also lifted his legs. Then he pushed with all his might. Three times he pushed, lifting the sky higher and higher until it was far off the ground.

The people of Earth straightened their backs and reached

their arms above their heads in amazement, for no ceiling held them down. From then on, people stood tall and could go about their daily tasks freely.

Some say, if it had not been for Maui, the sky would have fallen completely and humans could not have survived. So it is that Maui saved mankind and allowed them to stand tall.

CHAPTER 18

Holding their course through the night, Moana used everything Maui had taught her—sensing the wind on her face, tracking the stars as they rose and set, using the swells of the ocean to keep time.

From his seat in the bow, Maui shot her a proud look. A light began to glow, but it wasn't coming from the east. Looking down, Moana saw that her shell necklace was lit from within. The heart of Te Fiti was shining through the cracks.

Moana looked to Maui, who checked the horizon. There, in the distance, hung an angry mass of dark clouds. Beyond them, she saw the hint of land.

Moana turned questioning eyes to Maui, who nodded.

"Te Fiti," he confirmed.

Something white and fluffy drifted past her face and her nose tingled oddly. Looking around, she saw more little specks filling the air, landing on the boat and in Maui's hair, everywhere. Could this be snow? She'd heard tales of unseasonably cold storms whipping snow down from the mountains, but the air didn't feel cold.

A fleck landed on her arm, the grayish spot standing out against her brown skin. No, definitely not cold. Peering closer, Moana realized it was ash—which meant something was burning nearby.

As they drew closer to the clouds, she realized the source of the ash. To get to Te Fiti, they would have to cross through a ring of barrier islands—each one a blackened, jagged crag. Smoke seeped up from within them, hence the ash that hung over the ocean for miles around. The ominous circle of rocks almost seemed to be holding Te Fiti hostage.

Running a hand along the canoe's hull, Maui lifted up a pinch of ash and rubbed it between his thumb and forefinger, a frown creasing his face. His eyes narrowed in determination.

"It's Maui time," he said, his voice fierce.

Moana was impressed by his bravado.

Puffing up his chest, Maui strutted to the bow.

"Te Kā!" he bellowed, the call reverberating off the clouds of ash.

A shiver ran through Moana as a flare of red lit up one of the barrier islands and a thick plume of smoke roiled up into the sky. A menacing aura pervaded the air, and the hair on her arms prickled with alarm. Heihei popped up his head, took one look around, then ducked back down in the cargo hold. Maui's form wavered then steadied, proof that he was nervous, as well.

"You ready?" Moana asked.

"Huhn," Maui said, putting on his warrior face. But it was a bit lackluster.

"Huhn!" Moana shouted back, leaning close to him with a warrior face of her own.

"HUHN!" he yelled, his features pulled into a scary grimace.

Nodding in approval, Moana took the stone from her necklace and wrapped one of his hands around it. "Go save the world," she told him.

With a burst of feathers, Maui shifted into a hawk and launched off the boat, streaking toward Te Fiti.

"Cheeee-hoooo!" Moana called after him, her fist lifted into the sky.

Cheered by her cry, the hawk flew faster, zipping through the air. As he reached the outer islands, water crashed up in front of him with a hiss, steam and ash exploding in his path.

From the smoky cloud a fiery figure emerged, large as a mountain, deep cracks revealing the lava beneath the surface of its charred skin and allowing it to ooze out in orange flames. The monster's eyes and mouth burned in rage . . . and in a very literal fire as it screamed at Maui.

"Maui." Moana breathed his name in a whisper, suddenly understanding why the demigod had been so dubious about their chances before.

Maui banked up, trying to fly around the fiery creature, but Te Kā reared higher, filling the sky. Swinging a giant molten hand, the lava monster knocked Maui away.

"No!" Moana cried, watching her friend crumple and drop through the air. Grabbing the oar and loosening the main line, Moana tacked into the wind, racing toward him.

As Maui spiraled down, his powers seemed to waver—his feathers molting into skin, then scales, then back to skin as he smacked into the ocean. Leaning over, Moana hauled him aboard as she sailed past.

The demigod collapsed in the boat, sides heaving, clearly hurt, but as they headed straight for the barrier islands, he sat up in alarm.

"What are you doing?" he sputtered.

"Finding you a better way in!" Moana replied, her face set in determination.

Swinging the boom, Moana pivoted the boat through the water, aiming for a gap in the islands. But barreling along the rocks toward the same gap was the giant figure of Te Kā, the lava monster's hands stretched out in claws.

"We won't make it!" Maui cried, pointing to Te Kā.

Shaking her head, Moana gripped the oar tighter and tacked again. They had to make it—just a little bit farther and they'd be through. The wind was on their side, pushing them faster and faster.

Maui lunged up from the bottom of the canoe, reaching for the oar. "Turn around! Stop! Moana, *stop*!" he yelled.

They wrestled for the oar until finally Maui shouldered her aside. With a powerful thrust, he dug the oar into the sea, braking hard. The canoe spun sharply, throwing Moana against the hull. But it was too late. Te Kā was upon them.

Her arms flung over the side of the canoe, Moana watched in horror as Te Kā's monstrous fist slammed down toward them, the monster's face twisted vengefully. Paralyzed, Moana felt her heart skip. This was it. They weren't going to make it.

At the last moment, Maui surged up, flinging his hook over his head to block Te Kā.

BOOM! Fist and fishhook smashed together, the shock of the impact curling up massive tidal waves. The canoe rocketed to the top of one, riding it out to sea. Looking back, Moana could see Te Kā over the next crest of waves, lunging to follow, but something restrained the giant. Te Kā's arms scraped at the air as its body seemed trapped by an invisible force. Could Te Kā be tied to the barrier islands?

Whatever the reason, they left Te Kā behind, the ocean rolling them farther and farther out of reach.

CHAPTER 19

As the waves eased into their normal rhythm, Moana's heart slowly calmed down, as well. That had been close—so very close—and they were lucky to be alive. Moana looked around. The mast of the canoe was splintered, the wood ripped and top dangling down; the seams of the boat were cracked, and the edges of the sail smoldered, little embers rising into the night sky like stars. It looked no better than the run-down Kakamora boat they'd been using before.

If she hadn't tried to force them closer, if she hadn't tried to slip through the gap—if Maui hadn't been there to save them . . .

Moana turned to find the demigod hunched over, his head and shoulders slumped in defeat.

"Are you okay? Maui?" Moana edged closer,

worried. "Maui?"

What if he was really hurt?

The demigod turned and Moana felt a surge of relief, not seeing any bleeding . . . but then she saw the fishhook in his hands. Running down the center of it was an ugly deep crack.

"I told you to turn back," Maui said, his voice low. Tearing his eyes from the damaged hook, he looked up at her, his expression just as broken.

"I—I thought we could make it. . . ."

"We?" Maui asked, anger creeping into his tone.

Avoiding his piercing gaze, Moana studied the hook. "We can fix it," she said, sure there would be a solution. It would all be okay.

"It was made by the gods! You can't fix it," Maui snapped.

That stumped Moana for a minute as she mulled over his words. But she had an idea—the last image of Te Kā fresh in her mind.

"Next time we'll be more careful," she said. "Te Kā was stuck on the barrier islands. It's lava, it can't go in the water. We can find another way around."

Maui stared at her, his eyebrows pulled down in disbelief. "I'm not going back," he said, immovable.

"You still have to restore the heart," Moana argued.

"My hook is cracked. One more hit and it's over!" Maui raised the hook toward her, as if to remind her it was fractured.

"Maui, you have to restore the heart." They couldn't give up; there had to be a way.

"Without my hook, I'm nothing," he said.

"Maui—"

"WITHOUT MY HOOK, I AM *NOTHING*!" Maui bellowed.

Moana plopped backward in the boat, bowled over by his anger. Glaring at her, the demigod pulled out the heart of Te Fiti and dropped the stone on the floor of the canoe.

"Maui," Moana began, a nervous zing running through her. What was he doing? She stood up, blocking his way as he moved toward the bow, but he pushed past her easily. "Don't—we're only here because you stole the heart in the first place."

"We're here because the ocean told you you're special and you believed it," Maui countered, his words an angry hiss.

Stung, Moana bent to pick up the stone. Holding the warm spiral boosted her confidence. They had to complete their mission. She had to save her people.

"I am Moana of Motunui. You will board my boat—" she told him, steel in her voice.

"Good-bye, Moana," Maui cut in.

"—sail across the sea—" she continued, undeterred.

Maui shook his head. "I'm not killing myself so you can prove you're something you're not."

"—and restore the heart of Te Fiti!" Moana held up the spiral stone, her back straight. "The ocean chose me!"

Glancing at the heart, Maui turned away. "It chose wrong," he said.

Moana recoiled as if he'd slapped her, but before she could retort, feathers sprouted along his shoulders. . . . Then they faded out. His powers had really been shaken. With an angry grunt, Maui clutched his fishhook and morphed fully into a hawk, flying off into the night.

"Maui? *Maui!*" she yelled after him.

Despite the fact that, within a few minutes, Moana could no longer pick his shape out against the darkness, she continued to try, her eyes straining to detect any movement.

How could he have just run away like that? Didn't he feel responsible for setting things right? Would he come back when he calmed down? Were his powers really damaged?

As Moana started to replay what had happened, her stomach began to twist in guilt. Had she pushed him too hard? During the past couple of days, Maui had started to become, well, a *friend*—someone she could talk to and learn from. She had actually enjoyed her time with him. Maui hadn't felt ready to confront Te Kā and she'd wanted him to do so anyway. What kind of friend did that make her? Maybe he was right; maybe it was all her fault.

Sighing, Moana sank back on her knees, gazing down at the heart in her hands and gently brushing away the ash that dusted it. There was another thing that Maui could be right about—a question that really bothered her, causing a sensation like an itch on her back that she'd never be able to scratch.

Did he really think the ocean had made a mistake?

She looked out at the lapping waves. "Why did you bring me here?" she asked softly.

There was no response.

Cradling the heart of Te Fiti, Moana gazed at the sparkling spiral, wishing she knew what to do next. But as her eyes wandered over the shattered canoe, her heart twisted. She couldn't fix the boat, let alone save the world. Look what had happened when she'd seen Te Kā. She'd just barreled through, not giving any thought to what they were doing. Not listening to her friend when he'd clearly told her they couldn't make it.

Disappointment burned her throat and a wave of hopelessness crashed over her. Maybe Maui was right: maybe the ocean was crazy and its faith in her misplaced.

"You chose the wrong person," Moana whispered.

Leaning over the edge, she took one last look at the heart. She'd wanted to be worthy of it so much, but she'd failed. With a heavy heart, she held the stone out over the water.

"You have to choose someone else," she told the sea.

When nothing happened, she tried again. "Choose someone else!" Her plea grew more desperate, her voice louder. "Choose someone else!"

The only sound was the smacking of the waves against the hull, their rhythm unchanging.

"Please," Moana begged quietly. It was too much; she couldn't do it.

Finally, the water lifted up, curling around her

hand, almost as if it was about to cup her fingers closed around the stone and insist she keep it. But instead, the water wrapped around the heart and pulled it down into the sea. As the stone slipped beneath the waves, sinking down to the depths below, Moana felt wrenched apart. While she had feared she wasn't up to the job, a part of her had been hoping the ocean would refuse to accept it. She had *wanted* to have been the right choice.

Shoulders shaking, Moana slipped lower in the boat, her arms cradling her knees. What was she going to do now? Her eyes fell on her grandmother's necklace and she picked it up off her neck, rubbing the shiny shell. Gramma Tala had believed in her—had believed she could save them all, but instead Moana had let everyone down.

As Moana reached up to take off her necklace, a glimmer on the horizon caught her eye. Something big and glowing was streaking under the water toward her at an incredible pace.

Moana stood, peering at the shape. Was that—it was! A ghostly manta ray flew straight toward her. Passing under the boat, it turned and circled her a few times . . . then vanished.

No! Moana thought, leaning over the edge. *Please come back!*

"You're a long ways past the reef," someone said.

Whirling, Moana saw her grandmother perched on the bow of the canoe, a smile crinkling her face.

The Story of Fetuao and the Stars

ong ago, people sailed only in the light of day, relying on the sun to show them which way was north, south, east, or west. Voyagers had to stay within a half-day's sail, and everyone hurried home before night fell.

Fetuao chafed under those constraints and worried that a boat might be swept away in a storm and caught out past nightfall. Surely, *she thought*, there must be a means to travel by night. . . . After all, the moon and stars are bright.

Fetuao sat down to ponder, her eyes on the sky. Night after night, she watched the stars rise and traced their passage, but while the sun traveled in a straight arc over the world, the stars seemed to dance and weave, tripping here and there.

One evening, Fetuao climbed to the very top of a mountain to reach the sky. As the first star rose, Fetuao was there to greet it.

"Good evening," she said. "May I walk with you for a while?"

The star, which had lived a solitary life, was delighted to have company. "Of course you may!" it sang.

So Fetuao and the star walked together for an hour, talking of the beauty of night and the peacefulness of the waves below, and the star told Fetuao its name. All that time, Fetuao was taking note of their path, but soon the way was too steep for her.

"Dear star, thank you for letting me walk with you, but I'm afraid I cannot continue by your side any longer, for your road is too high," Fetuao said to the star.

"Yes, this is true," the star replied. "But I come close to earth again as I set. I hope we can meet then so that we can walk and talk together, for I have greatly enjoyed our time."

Fetuao agreed to meet the star as it was setting and waved good-bye as it rose out of reach. Then she hurried back to the horizon and greeted another star as it rose up.

"Dear star," she said. "You shine so brightly. I was hoping I might walk with you for a while and watch you glow."

Like the first star, the second one was all too happy to have some company, and again Fetuao walked with it, learning its name and which path it preferred, until it climbed too high in the sky.

"Dear star," Fetuao said. "I must leave you now, for I cannot follow where you go."

"Well, I hope we shall meet again," the star replied.

"If you will let me, I will join you as you set, when you are once again within my reach."

"That would be delightful," said the star. "I will look for you then."

Fetuao waved, then again returned to the horizon to meet another star. She continued this way for hours, until it was time to reunite with the first star on the far horizon. Hurrying, Fetuao arrived just as the first star slid into range.

"Ah, there you are!" cried the star. "I have been thinking of you all through the night and have so much to tell you."

Fetuao and the star walked until the star slid beyond the horizon, then she went back to accompany each of the other stars she'd met. It had been a long night, so Fetuao slept all the next day.

The following night, Fetuao again went to the sky and walked with more stars, learning their names and their stories. It took a year of nocturnal journeys, but after that, Fetuao knew all the stars and could trace their rising and setting with ease.

Coming down from the mountain, Fetuao passed along what she had learned to all the navigators. From then on, voyagers could sail far into the distance, unafraid of time, for once the sun sank below the waves, their new guiding lights—the stars—would come out one by one, and the wayfinders could greet them all by name.

CHAPTER 20

"**Gramma?**" Moana asked wonderingly. Was she really there?

Gramma Tala beamed at her then leaned forward. "Well, you just gonna sit there?"

Overwhelmed with emotion, Moana scrambled over to her, collapsing against her grandmother. Gramma Tala didn't feel as solid as she used to, as though there were more air under her skin, but Moana still felt warmth spreading through her as her grandmother's arms wrapped around her and her hands brushed through Moana's hair.

"I tried, Gramma, I—I couldn't do it." Moana hiccuped, tears welling in her eyes.

"It's not your fault," Gramma Tala reassured her. "I never should have put so much on your shoulders."

Gently, she brushed away Moana's tears, her fingers soft against Moana's cheeks. "If you are ready to go home, I will be with you."

With a sad nod, Moana picked up her oar and started to lower it into the ocean, but something stopped her. She stared at the oar. Who would save her island and her people if Moana returned home now? What would become of Motunui?

"Why do you hesitate?" Gramma Tala asked.

"I don't know." Moana felt overwhelmed by emotions—too many to pinpoint or explain.

"My love, you have always been different—and I *know* different." Moana gave a small smile as her grandmother continued. "You love the ocean. You love your people. And now, look at all that you have done because of those two loves. But there is something missing. . . ." She peered into her granddaughter's eyes. "Do you know who you are?"

Moana frowned, shaking her head slightly.

"Hit the drum and listen to the voice inside you. What does it say?" Gramma Tala asked.

Looking back and forth between her grandmother and the drum, which had miraculously remained intact after their run-in with Te Kā, Moana slowly made her way over to it and knelt down. Her hands hovered before she brought them down—*thump!* "Who am I? I am a villager from the island of Motunui. I am the daughter of a great chief. I am a girl who loves where I come from, who loves my family, who loves my people."

Moana stared up at the stars and at the ocean around her, thinking about her ancestors. She banged the drum again, a little stronger this time. "I am a girl who loves the sea. I am a descendent of great voyagers. I am a wayfinder. I am a leader of my people," she declared, banging the drum more forcefully.

Nodding, Gramma Tala motioned for her to go on.

"I am a warrior," Moana added, striking the drum again. "I am a girl who has been on a great journey—befriending demigods, battling monsters. I have been changed by what I have done, by what I have learned." She pounded out a deep boom.

Moana paused, suddenly realizing she knew what her grandmother was trying to teach her. She took a deep breath, letting all her fears and doubts fall away. There was still more for her to do, more for her to learn. She needed to let go of all expectations for who she should be. She smiled, realizing who she truly was—in every fiber of her being, her heart, and her spirit—and accepted herself completely.

Banging on the drum, Moana shouted up to the sky: "I am Moana!"

Gramma Tala's smile was wide and her eyes twinkled with pride.

BOOM! Moana pounded the drum.

BOOM! An answering drumbeat came from deep within the ocean and then a fleet of voyaging canoes burst forth from beneath the waves, the glowing spirits of her ancestors on board.

The spectral boats flanked her, spreading out on either side, with her canoe in the lead. Seeing her ancestors all around her sent a tingle of awe through Moana. Their voices sang out, reminding her to be true to herself. She was a wayfinder like them, a warrior, and a proud leader. She was Moana, and she belonged exactly where she was—in the prow of her canoe.

Moana could see a light far beneath the waves. The heart was down there, waiting for her. Her experiences had shaped her, the people she loved changed her, her ancestors guided her, but she was more than the sum of those parts. She just had to believe in herself.

Glowing brightly, Gramma Tala leaned her

forehead against Moana's, lighting up her face.

"Know who you are, Moana," she whispered fiercely. "Always know who you are."

Moana glanced at the fathomless waves, then back to her grandmother with a smile. She was ready to claim her destiny. Standing up on the bow, she took one last look at Gramma Tala and dove gracefully into the sea.

Cool water surrounded her, the darkness complete. Moana pulled herself lower, sensing more than seeing which direction was downward. Far below, a light sparked, glowing brighter and brighter. Kicking her legs in wide arcs, she propelled herself toward it, ignoring the stitch in her side.

Her lungs began to squeeze, the pressure of the water building the deeper she went, and her fingers and toes felt numb in the cold, but Moana struggled on, determined to reach the glowing orb. Down and down, she was so close now, just a few more feet . . . Her lungs felt like they were on fire, burning with the need to take in air.

Stretching her fingers out as far as she could, Moana brushed them against the heart of Te Fiti, digging it out of the sandy ocean floor. Turning, she kicked off with a powerful thrust and zoomed toward the surface.

Splash! Moana broke through the ceiling of the sea to find the sky a beautiful purple as dawn approached. Her grandmother and the spirits of her ancestors were gone, the waves empty, but Moana smiled down at her fist, where the heart of Te Fiti glowed softly.

Climbing back aboard her canoe, Moana secured the heart inside her necklace, then turned to survey the damage to the boat. On closer inspection, she saw the mast could be fixed, the outrigger reassembled.

She could do this. She could return the heart herself. She had a plan.

"I am Moana of Motunui. Aboard my boat, I will sail across the sea . . . and restore the heart of Te Fiti!" she proclaimed as she set about putting her boat back together.

"Bowk-bowk!" Heihei squawked, bobbing his head up and down.

Working steadily as the sky lightened, Moana wove new ropes from coconut threads and sealed the cracks in the hull. She ran her hands over the sail, testing its strength, then tightened a line, swung the boom, and hoisted the sailcloth high. Heihei flapped to the top of the mast, the wind ruffling his feathers as it filled the sail.

Ready to go, Moana charted the course, lowered her oar, and adjusted the sail, and the boat soared over the waves.

As the sun rose over the horizon, Moana sailed through a thin mist, the cool droplets refreshing on her skin. The wind gusted, helping her boat slice quickly through the water and skim over the swells. Looking ahead, Moana spotted the dark, ominous ring of the barrier islands encircling Te Fiti. She knew Te Kā was there somewhere.

Moana slowed her boat as she approached, swinging parallel to study the craggy rocks until she found a gap wide enough for her canoe.

For all his dimwittedness, Heihei must have recognized the foreboding aura that hung around the area. *"Bowk?"* he squawked tentatively.

Moana shot him a reassuring smile. "Te Kā can't follow us into the water. We make it past the barrier islands, we make it to Te Fiti," she told him, going over her plan aloud. He stared back at her blankly. "None of which you understand because you are a chicken."

Picking Heihei up, she placed him carefully in a basket where he couldn't wander off into the sea. Next Moana wrapped one hand around the heart and took a deep breath. Then she pulled the sail line tight, steering toward the gap in the barrier islands. A thick pillar of ash hung over the gap—and there was Te Kā, waiting for her.

Totally focused, Moana kept the sail tight and her eyes on the gap as they got closer and closer. Suddenly, she leaned her weight back, counterbalancing the force of the wind, and used her body to flip the boat in the opposite direction, aiming for a different gap.

Te Kā's eyes narrowed in anger and the lava monster raced along the rocks to the other gap, hurling balls of molten lava at Moana to slow her down.

Bam! Splash!

Moana had to tack frequently, angling the boat back and forth to avoid the lava. Despite the plumes of steam and ash erupting each time the lava collided with the water, Moana was getting closer.

Seeing this, Te Kā smashed its fiery hands together, creating a massive blazing ball, then launched it toward the gap itself. A huge cloud of steam billowed up as the lava crashed down into the water, filling the space and fusing the islands together. The gap was impassible now. The lava monster had blocked the path.

But as the steam cleared, Te Kā leaned back in

surprise. Moana had disappeared. Whirling, Te Kā spotted Moana's boat almost back to the first gap. She had doubled back!

From her place in the stern, Moana grinned, happy her plan was working. Te Kā would never make it back to the first gap in time.

But Te Kā wasn't going to give up that easily. The lava monster lunged downward, pushing at the islands themselves. With a tremendous groan of rock against rock, the islands began to move, shifting to close the gap.

Huge boulders, dislodged by the force of Te Kā's push, began to rain down, tumbling into the ocean all around Moana. Shoved sideways by the crash of a nearby boulder, Moana lost her grip on the main line. Dismay filled her as the rope flew through the air, but with a quick lunge, Heihei grabbed the end of it in his beak.

Stunned, Moana stared at the rooster as he tugged the line back to her. The splash of a steaming boulder jarred her back to the present. Yanking on the rope, she sliced through the water, the canoe tilting to take full advantage of the wind—and they were through the gap just in time.

BOOM! A crag of an island broke off and crashed

into the gap, sealing it shut. The resulting wave pushed Moana toward Te Fiti and she raised her hand in victory.

"We did it! We—" Moana cried, then cut off. Where was Heihei?

Turning, she saw him floundering in the water near the now-blocked gap. He must have been knocked off the boat by a rock.

"Heihei," Moana called.

Despite the fact that she was so close to her goal, the sand of Te Fiti just a few hundred feet away, Moana didn't hesitate. It was her responsibility to take care of him. Swinging the boat around, she rocketed back toward the rooster and plucked him from the waves.

With a whoosh of smoke and ash, Te Kā reared up from the islands nearby and smacked the canoe into the air. Moana, Heihei, and the boat all flew up, spinning end over end, before plunging into the unnaturally warm seawater, heated by proximity to Te Kā's angry form.

Her limbs flailing under the water, Moana twisted to find the surface, narrowly avoiding the rocks Te Kā was showering down on her. Gasping, she surfaced, then kicked over to Heihei, who was splashing nearby.

After plonking him on her head, she pulled herself to her overturned canoe and set a bedraggled Heihei on the upside-down hull.

Moana took a deep breath, then swam under and tried to pull the mast up to roll the canoe back, but the outrigger provided too much resistance. She couldn't right it that way.

Unhooking the sail, she grabbed hold of the mast line, surfaced, and circled to the windward side of the boat. Leaning over the hull of the canoe, she set her feet on its outer edge and used her body weight to tip the boat back toward her slowly, pulling on the line at the same time. Heihei scrabbled along next to her as the hull rolled.

She was poised halfway up the hull, the mast now resting on the surface of the ocean, when she felt a shadow loom over her. Glancing up, she saw Te Kā, who looked more enraged than ever. Before Moana could fling herself back into the water, Te Kā's fist slammed toward her.

There was nothing Moana could do to escape. Squeezing her eyes shut, she braced for the blow.

BOOM!

The Story of
the Wind Sisters

he Sky and Earth gave birth to four wind daughters: East, North, South, and West. East Wind was the strong, steady daughter who could be relied upon to do as she was asked, although when her parents turned their backs, she pushed hard to get her own way. North and South Wind were somewhat temperamental. At times they were cool and aloof, but at other times they were warm and friendly. As for West Wind, she was a flighty young thing, easily distracted.

Despite the fact that they loved each other dearly, the sisters often quarreled. One day, East Wind returned to her room to find her favorite shell necklace in pieces on the floor.

"Who broke my necklace?" East Wind cried out angrily. "Was it you, North?"

"Not I! I have been busy in the garden all morning," North replied. She showed her sister her dirt-covered hands as proof.

Scowling, East turned to South. "Was it you, South? Did you break my necklace?"

Immediately offended, for she was in a terrible mood already, South huffed impatiently: "I have not touched your necklace. Although if I had broken it, it would only be fair considering you have stolen my favorite resting spot under the palm tree for the past week and I have been forced to sleep in the hot sun instead."

"There are plenty of other shade-covered spots," East retorted. "It is not my fault you are too slow when it comes time to rest."

Before South could reply, East stormed over to the window, where West was sitting, staring out at the mountains with a dreamy look in her eye.

"West, did you play with my necklace?" East asked, holding up the shattered pieces.

West blinked slowly out of her daze and turned to East with a smile. "No, sister, I did not. Perhaps it fell by accident?"

"It was no accident," East said, annoyed that none of her sisters would confess. "It was one of you!"

"How dare you accuse us?" South yelled.

"I told you, I have been working tirelessly all morning!" North cried at the same time.

All day the sisters raged at one another, stirring up old wounds and flinging harsh words. Their argument grew so loud that the Sky and Earth had to cover their ears.

"Enough!" bellowed the Sky when he could take it no more. "If you cannot sort this out peacefully, we will separate you. Each of you go to the ends of the horizon and stay there."

So the East, North, South, and West Winds swept off to the four corners of the horizon and sat down. To keep them busy, the Earth and Sky gave each of them a giant fan. East, North, and South waved their fans, each wanting to have their say by pushing the air toward the others. But West frolicked and played in the water and only remembered to take up her fan once a year when East took a rest and West no longer felt her sister's wind on her face.

That is why the voyagers must wait for the time every year when the East Wind rests and the West Wind finally blows in order to explore the sea far to the east. No matter how far they go, they know that the winds will change in time and the East Wind can carry them home again.

CHAPTER 21

White light flashed around her and a shock wave rocked Moana and the boat, but she could feel the coarse rope in her hands and smell the saltwater in the air. Her eyes popped open. She was still alive. Above her she saw Maui, his hook raised to block Te Kā's fist.

"Maui?" Moana cried in surprise.

As Te Kā retreated to the top of an atoll to gather strength, Maui dropped down to Moana's overturned boat.

"But your hook—" Moana said, seeing it was still cracked.

Maui hefted the hook, a crooked smile on his face. "Yeah, I talked it over with a buddy of mine." He glanced down at Mini Maui, who was nodding sagely.

"I have some abandonment and self-worth issues I'm working on and—"

Whoosh! A fireball shot past them, barely missing the canoe.

"Another time. I got your back, Chosen One. Go save the world," Maui urged. He and Moana quickly righted her boat fully. Moana climbed aboard with Heihei, and Maui moved to transform.

"Wait, Maui," Moana called, stopping him. Joy and gratitude were bubbling through Moana. She smiled at him, glad he was there and glad he'd realized he didn't need his hook at full power to be a hero. It was *trying* that made him one.

"Thank you," she said, meaning it with every fiber of her being and realizing it was the first time she had said those words to him.

Maui beamed. "You're welcome," he said.

The fishhook glowed as he summoned its power then flew into the air as a hawk, zooming toward Te Kā.

Moana ran to unfurl the sail. With a series of quick shifts of the oar, Moana deftly avoided the lava cascading from Te Kā's hands while Maui did his part to keep the lava monster occupied, diving and circling Te Kā.

Te Kā pulled back a molten arm to swing at Moana, but Maui was faster. Speeding down, he landed on the lava monster's arm and rapidly transformed into a mulititude of animals—shark, whale, lizard—quickly scampering across Te Kā's skin and distracting it from Moana.

"Hot-hot-hot-hot-hot!" he cried.

Te Kā shook him off, and he transformed back into a hawk in midair, screeching in defiance. Using the hook, he sliced off one of the lava monster's hands. Te Kā reared back in rage. With one powerful punch, Te Kā knocked Maui into a crag of one of the barrier islands.

Te Kā's molten hand was already growing back. The lava monster turned toward Moana, preparing a massive fireball and aiming it at her canoe. Moana tried to steer away, but it was no use. She would not be able to get out of the line of fire. She braced herself for the impact and felt the ocean push her forward, trying to help.

BAM!

The boat shattered, flinging Moana into the water. Moana gasped for air, her boat in fragments all around her. Heihei clung to a small piece of the canoe, staying afloat. Moana treaded water, taking in all the damage. This time it looked like her boat was beyond repair. But there was no time to think about that at the moment. She looked toward the island in front of her. There was a shift in the current, and a wave rapidly pushed her to it.

As soon as she reached the shallows, Moana scrambled up the rocky edge, pumping her legs as fast as she could.

Furious, Te Kā made another fireball and prepared to throw it at Moana. From the barrier island, Maui lurched to his feet, realizing the danger. He and Mini Maui exchanged a look before Maui swung his fishhook over his head, leaping up into the sky to block Te Kā. White light exploded from the impact.

At the same time, Moana charged up the tall cliffs, then halted abruptly, her stomach dropping at the sight before her eyes.

"No," she said, the word a tight exhale.

There was no spiral there. Moana was standing at the edge of a massive crater, the pit filled with water . . . the rest of the island just . . . gone.

"Te Fiti—it's gone," Moana said.

Moana turned, unsure what to do. Where could

she place the heart? She saw Te Kā looming over Maui, the monster's face clenched in anger. As Maui got to his feet, Moana could see that his fishhook had been completely shattered. Chips of white fragments lay all around him.

Yet Maui didn't stop to grieve. Quickly scaling the crag, he braced himself on a plateau and started doing a warrior dance, taunting Te Kā and keeping the lava monster's attention on him. He wasn't going to let Te Kā get in Moana's way.

Moana watched helplessly as Te Kā stormed toward Maui, volcanic eruptions bursting out from the creature's fiery hair, clawed fingers reaching for the demigod. Te Kā reared back to strike a fatal blow. On the lava monster's chest, Moana could just pick out a faded spiral shape, crusted over.

"The spiral," Moana whispered, glancing back and forth between the crater where Te Fiti used to be and the angry, fiery monster trapped on the barrier islands. Unclasping the shell of her necklace, Moana pulled out the heart of Te Fiti and let it rest on her palm, where it began to glow.

"Know who you are," Moana said slowly. What if Te Kā was really somebody else entirely? Somebody who had lost their way when the heart of Te Fiti was stolen? What if Te Kā *was* the goddess Te Fiti? The lava monster did seem to be guarding the remnants of the island.

When Moana looked to the ocean for confirmation, it seemed to nod in choppy approval. Holding the heart high, Moana let it shine brightly out toward the barrier islands. The flash of white light caught Te Kā's eye and the lava monster stopped mid-swing.

At the edge of the ocean, Moana gestured to the waves. "Let her come to me," she told it. The water parted before her in a canyon that reached from the sandy crater out to the barrier islands.

Maui struggled to his feet, confused. "Moana, what are you doing?" he shouted.

With a clear passageway to Moana, Te Kā rushed toward her. Moana headed toward her on the same path, undaunted, a calmness settling over her. She was not afraid; she knew what she had to do. When Te Kā was deep within the canyon, Moana looked to the ocean on either side, then began to speak. "I've come a long way to see you."

Nearly upon her, Te Kā rose to its full height, ready to attack, but Moana stood her ground and kept going. "I know that sometimes the world tries to take things away from you. Sometimes it tries to take what makes you special. And that's hard. But it's the hard things, the scars that help shape us." Te Kā paused, listening. Moana continued, "I know what it's like to feel incomplete. And I can help if you, if you let me. I know there's still a voice inside. Nothing can ever take that voice away. You just have to stop and listen. *Listen to the voice inside you.*" Her grandmother's words seemed to soothe Te Kā and the lava monster slowly shrank, lowering its head to regard Moana. Gently, Moana leaned forward, touching her forehead to Te Kā's blackened one in a *hongi*.

"Know who you are," Moana whispered, slotting the stone into the spiral shape on Te Kā's chest.

Vibrations shook Moana as Te Kā's skin began to crack, the rocky surface splintering and falling away to reveal a peaceful green face. Moana had been right: Te Kā was really Te Fiti.

The heart stone glowed brightly, then light flowed out to fill in the spiral shape on Te Fiti's chest. As the lava and ash fell away, a woven crown of emerald leaves and vibrant flowers emerged on Te Fiti's head. The barrier islands sank away, leaving Maui treading water.

Whoosh!

The ocean wrapped around Maui and sucked him toward the shore, depositing him on the sand next to Moana and Heihei with a thump.

CHAPTER 22

"**The chicken lives!**" Maui shouted, scooping up Heihei into a hug. The rooster squawked indignantly, unsure why he was so high in the air all of a sudden, and wriggled free.

Moana felt the ground shift underneath her and she and Maui were lifted up on a hand of earth. The serene face of Te Fiti peered down at them and Moana quickly knelt, tugging Maui down next to her.

Solemnly, Te Fiti nodded her thanks to Moana for restoring her heart. Moana nodded back, her own heart singing in her chest.

Te Fiti swung her gaze to Maui, who shrugged sheepishly.

"Hey there, Te Fiti," he said, attempting to be charming. "So . . . how ya been?"

An awkward pause ensued and Maui shifted uncomfortably.

"Look, what I did was . . . I have no excuse. I did it for myself and—and I'm sorry." The demigod hung his head penitently, his voice sincere. "You may smite me now."

For a long moment, Te Fiti merely studied him as though she were weighing his good deeds against his misdeeds. Then her expression softened and she reached out her other hand, unfurling her fingers.

In the center of her palm lay Maui's fishhook, the white bone glistening as though it had never been cracked. Te Fiti extended her hand toward Maui, letting him take the hook back.

"YES! CHEEE-HOO—" Maui caught himself, reining in his enthusiasm. "Thank you, thank you. Your kind gesture is deeply, deeply appreciated," he finished politely. He looked from Te Fiti to Moana, shifting uncomfortably. "I'm just gonna—" He swished the hook and transformed into a beetle, hovering in the air. "Take your time, I'll be down there," he told Moana, before flying away.

Shaking her head slightly, Te Fiti turned her attention to Moana and lowered her forehead to give her another *hongi*. Moana felt honored at the exchange of breath with the beautiful mother island. Energy and lightness flowed through her. Pulling back, Te Fiti lowered Moana to the shore and drew out her arm to indicate the seas were open and waiting for them to explore.

Then, with a smile and a gentle wave, Te Fiti vanished into the earth. Softly rounded mountains rose up to replace the crater as the island of Te Fiti was reborn, bursting with life. Vibrantly colored fruit dripped down from the trees, the scent of flowers wafted through the air as blossoms opened up, and the songs of birds and insects could be heard from within the shaded forest. An explosion of flower petals whirled through the air, swirling on the shore and revealing Moana's canoe in the shallow water. Moana gasped. Her beloved boat was fully restored and covered in flowers, the pinks, reds, purples, yellows, and blues floating down around them like a colored rainstorm.

Moana rushed over to it, meeting Maui, now in his human shape, at the water's edge.

"Bowk-bowk!" Heihei squawked nearby, seemingly oblivious to all that had just transpired. Moana smiled

at the little rooster, and Maui set out some birdseed for him. "I'm gonna miss you, drumstick," he teased. As Heihei lunged for the seed and missed, Maui added: "Don't ever change."

Moana and Maui exchanged grins. Then Moana frowned slightly. They had done it; they had returned the heart of Te Fiti. It was the end of the journey, and it was time to say good-bye. She could feel it. She looked to the horizon, trying to think of the words that would be able to express her gratitude, her pride in being his friend.

But Maui spoke first, gesturing toward the sea. "You know, the ocean used to love when I pulled up islands, because someone would sail her seas to find 'em. Every day a new village on this island, a new village on that one. And the water connected them all."

He turned back to her. "If I were the ocean," he speculated, "I'd be looking for a shortish curly-haired non-princess to start that again."

Moana smiled broadly, feeling a slight lump in her throat. Just then, Maui tapped his chest; a new tattoo was forming over his heart. In the ink, Moana saw a mini Moana aboard a boat, pointing the way over the waves—looking every bit a proud wayfinder. Next to the scene, Mini Maui smiled at Moana, then lifted the tattoo sky, settling into place.

Maui swung his hook over his head, charging up its powers, but before he could transform, Moana leapt forward and threw her arms around him, squeezing tight. Touched, Maui returned her hug, then morphed into hawk form.

Circling the canoe once as Moana hoisted the sail, he swooped his wings in farewell, then soared up into the clouds. It was the perfect good-bye.

With the island of Te Fiti at her back and nothing but open ocean between her and Motunui, Moana picked up her oar and settled into the canoe, her eyes alight. It was time to go home.

The Story of
Maui Going Fishing

After helping Moana restore the heart of Te Fiti, Maui, demigod of wind and sea, hero of men and women, was overjoyed to receive his magical fishhook back from Te Fiti. Without his fishhook, Maui had been a brave warrior and a loyal friend, but with it, Maui felt unstoppable. He could transform into any shape, battle any monster, even cut a cliff in half if he so chose.

What shall I do next? *Maui wondered as he soared through the air. Wind streamed in under his wings, lifting him higher. He loved his hawk form, loved being so free, able to swoop and spin in the air, nothing around him for miles but some drifting white clouds and a pure blue sky.*

Below him, the ocean waves stretched far into the distance, their dark blue color a sign of just how deep the water lay. As much as he loved being aloft, it would be nice to rest his wings for a while.

Maui's sharp eyes scanned the sea and then the sky until he spotted land. Banking to the right, Maui winged down to the island, glad to see it vibrant with life—the plants a bold array of emerald, jade, and lime green.

As he explored, Maui was struck by a desire to go fishing, so *he fashioned a canoe from one of the sturdy trees. Paddling out, Maui got farther and farther from the island until it was only a speck on the horizon.*

He gazed around at the beautiful vista, then cast his fishhook overboard, letting out the line attached to it. Deeper and deeper the hook sank, dropping into the cold depths of the sea. Maui whistled a song to himself to pass the time until— tug—he'd snagged something!

Leaping up, Maui grabbed hold of the line with two hands and hauled it up. It was harder than he'd expected.

"Chee-hooo!" he cried, full of mana.

His muscles strained at the weight. It had to be the largest fish Maui had ever caught—maybe even the largest fish anyone had ever caught.

Hand over hand, Maui wrestled with the line, yanking it in bit by bit. Peering overboard, he could see something rising from the depths and he felt a thrill of excitement.

Moments later, a sharp jagged point broke through the waves, followed by a mountain, Maui's hook wedged tightly in one of the rocky crags. Maui secured his line and began to row, pulling up more and more of the island as he went. Smaller mountains followed, then valleys, waterfalls, and forests leading down to a softly curving beach.

Pausing, Maui admired his work. The island was magnificent. He grinned as he thought about Moana and her people finding this island on their next voyage. Then Maui retrieved his fishhook from the mountain and sailed on, eager to pull up more islands from the ocean floor. He would sail south and north and east, creating island after island for the voyagers to discover.

They could all thank him later. Right then he had some fishing to do.

CHAPTER 23

Giant green peaks rose from the horizon as though Moana had summoned them just by picturing them. Heihei turned from his place at the bow to squawk at Moana.

"Yes, that's Motunui," Moana told him, feeling a thrill of pride. Using everything Maui had taught her, she'd done it: she'd followed the stars, listened to the winds, watched the clouds, and felt the waves to find her way home.

As she piloted through a gap in the reef, leaving behind the deeper waters for the lagoon, she heard the trumpet of a conch shell from shore. Her heart thrummed nervously, but she held her back straight and tugged on the sail line to tack into the inlet.

Clustered on the beach, the people stared in shock

as Moana guided her canoe right up to the edge of the village. Moana splashed over the side and waded ashore, anchoring her boat in the shallows, then turned to face the villagers.

Moana's mother rushed forward and swept her into a tight embrace, Chief Tui close behind her, a parade of emotions flickering in his eyes: relief, love, regret, and pride. As Sina stepped back, Tui took her place, crushing Moana in a powerful hug, spinning her like he had when she was a little girl.

In this gesture, Moana could feel that her father was accepting her for who she was and was proud of what she had done.

As he set her down, she wiped a tear from his cheek. She had missed him, too, and couldn't wait to tell him of all her adventures.

"Snort, snort!" Hooves pawed at Moana's legs.

"Pua!" Moana exclaimed, stooping down to give the pig a hug. Pua lunged up, licking her face excitedly. "Whoa, snout in the mouth!" Moana laughed, wiping her lips.

"Wheee!" Several kids squealed happily as they ran down to the water. Splashing and laughing, they clambered aboard Moana's canoe and began playing with the oar and drum. One stood in the bow of the boat, arm extended, pretending to lead the way.

From under the shade of a coconut tree, Moana stood with her mother and watched as her father waded into the water, as well, and circled the canoe, both impressed and pensive as he studied the boat. Coming to join them, he nodded in pride.

"You have done well, Moana," he said, draping an arm around her shoulders.

Pleased, Moana leaned against him, but she straightened as a mighty gust blew her hair around her face. The wind had changed. . . . It was flowing east.

Moana's father's eyes followed as her gaze swept across the inlet to where the sky touched the sea in a bold line, then they both looked toward the cavern of ancient boats. Without words, he knew what her heart was yearning for and he gave her a little squeeze of assent.

. . . .

"Slowly, slowly, nice and easy," Moana coached as the row of villagers heaved on the rope, pulling the double-hulled canoe out into the sun.

Several more boats lined the beach, carpenters

already hard at work repairing the hulls, their hammer beats echoed by bangs from the village as another crew flattened cloth for a new sail.

Kids raced up and down the beach, fetching ropes and tools, while Moana's mother led several women in the harvesting and packing of food. Out on the lagoon, Tui was giving sailing lessons.

With a soft swish, the double-hulled canoe slid across the sand to take its place in the line. In a well-practiced dance, the villagers anchored it and began sanding it down.

Convinced that the boats were in good hands, Moana stepped back. It had been impressive how quickly everyone had embraced the idea of restoring the canoes and sailing east to find new islands. *Perhaps I was not the only one in the village with an itch to explore,* she thought with a smile.

The waves lapped around her ankles and something firm knocked into her. Looking down, Moana laughed in delight. It was a conch shell, the very same shell the ocean had offered her when she was a toddler. Moana picked it up, the smooth, warm curve of it familiar in her hands. She knew exactly what to do with it.

• • • • • • • • • • • •

From the summit of Motunui, the canoes looked like toys poised on the edge of the sea, the island itself a giant boat floating in the midst of the vast ocean. Wind whipped through Moana's hair as she rounded the corner and stopped before the pillar of rocks.

This was where her ancestors, all the chiefs before her, had come to honor the island and their people, raising them higher to the sky. Each one had left a stone to represent who he was, both as a leader and for himself . . . and now it was Moana's turn.

Carefully, Moana balanced her choice on the top of the pile. Above, a ray of sunlight pierced through the clouds and danced over the spikes of the conch shell, the pearly coral surface gleaming against the blue sky.

• • • • • • • • • • • • •

White-capped waves splashed under Moana, lifting her canoe as it cut through the water. Above, the sailcloth flapped then snapped tight, capturing the wind. Wild with excitement to be back on the water, Moana leaned over the edge, feeling the breeze tug at her.

In the bow, Pua had his snout raised to the sky,

and Heihei had assumed his usual perch on the masthead. Moana glanced to the side, her gaze taking in her parents on a boat of their own, some of the other villagers standing on board a fleet of boats, their decks brimming with supplies, the people basking in the sun. They were excited to go exploring, to see what lay beyond the reef. Looking ahead, Moana saw the outline of a giant manta ray gliding before her canoe and she touched Gramma Tala's necklace, still clasped around her neck.

Screeaaww! A massive hawk dove out of the sky, slicing the water in front of her canoe. Grinning at the sight of Maui, Moana tugged on the main line and rode the wake from the demigod's claws. Wind whipped her hair back and she lifted her face to the sky.

Together, her people were reclaiming their place as voyagers, with Moana to lead them. She felt no fear as they sailed into the unknown. She knew where she came from, she knew who she was, and she was ready.

The ocean was her home, the waves and winds her friends, the sun and stars her guiding lights.

The Story of
Moana the Wayfinder

 long time ago, there were great voyagers. They rode the waves, captured the four winds, knew the stars by name, and read the clouds from one end of the sea to another. Then the heart of Te Fiti was stolen, resulting in a time of darkness—the waters stalked by monsters—and people retreated to the safety of the island, forgetting the ways of their ancestors.

Many years later, a child was born with the sea in her spirit. Her name was Moana, and sensing the goodness and strength in her, the ocean entrusted her with a special mission: to restore the heart of Te Fiti and thereby stop the spreading darkness.

Leaving behind all she knew, Moana crossed the reef and found the demigod Maui. Together they voyaged to Lalotai, the realm of monsters, and battled a giant crab to retrieve Maui's magical fishhook. As they sailed for Te Fiti, Maui taught Moana all he knew of the lost art of wayfinding, showing her the tools her ancestors had used, while Moana helped him regain control of his mighty powers.

When they reached the mother island, Maui and Moana were confronted by the terrifying Te Kā. Maui tried to battle the fire monster, but Moana looked deeper. She could see *something no one else could. She sang to Te Kā. With the return of her heart, Te Kā was transformed back into her true self: the goddess Te Fiti.*

The darkness turned to light, and the islands were returned to their former lush and vibrant states. Thankful, Te Fiti welcomed Moana and her people to travel the seas and voyage to her shores again. With the wind blowing in her hair, Moana sailed back to her home island, where her people were waiting to celebrate her return. Now a master wayfinder, Moana taught her people to sail the seas once again, ushering in a new era of exploration, restoring her people to their rightful place on the waves. Together, they set forth to explore the ocean that connected them to all the islands and to take home tales of their own adventures.

They were proud. They were free. They were voyagers.